Wynter Chronicles

Wynter Chronicles

MANYA BHANSALI

NU VOICE
PRESS

First published by NU VOICE PRESS 2024
An imprint of Hubhawks Pvt. Ltd
www.nuvoicepress.com

This is a work of fiction and all characters and incidents described in this book are the product of the author's imagination. Any resemblance to actual persons, living or dead, is entirely coincidental.

ISBN: 978-81-970218-5-5

Typeset by Saanvi Graphics, Noida
Printed at Nutech Print Services - India
Published by Nu Voice Press

To my little cutie, Nabz,
who begged and begged until I finally let him see
my first draft.
This one's for you, lil bro.

"Around ten millennia ago, in the year 3050, the foulest thing one could have imagined happened. The Chaliz activated the earthquakes.

Do you ever wonder why earthquakes happen?

The Chaliz, a bull-dog-like creature, only 100 times larger, with bloodshot eyes, used to live in Earth's core where all the once-called fantasy creatures lived. The Chaliz would sleep for many centuries at a time. When he would wake up, every step he took produced loud thuds on Earth's surface. That was the real reason earthquakes formed.

The problem occurred when a winged cat woke the Chaliz up in the middle of his sleep. The winged cat waking up the bull-dog-like creature was an abysmal idea. He got so infuriated, he started chasing her. While chasing her, the Chaliz caused so much destruction to Earth's core, and the whole surface as well, that the world blasted like a bomb. The only part of Earth that remained was a small island. That is what, according to scientists, caused the World Bomb.

Only two people survived the World Bomb — Edward Rev and Rowana King. Edward and Rowana had nine children. The future generations..."

Mum used to read this bedtime story to Kelly and me, before we slept. She said her mom used to read it to her when she was little. I would listen to the story as Mum read it to my little brothers, Andy and Archie, though they pretended to sleep early so they didn't have to listen to any more of it. Kelly would find it rude because she was always about 'Mama Manners', but I found it cute.

Two years ago...

-1-

A Normal Day

The thunder thrived as the dark grey clouds wept out rain droplets and mist clouded the atmosphere. Dew dripped from the windows of the snoozing buildings. The monotonous moon's colour drained. The voice of the footsteps resonated from far off. Right in the center of the inclement night stood two men, wrestling each other. One was a short man, wearing a plain, black mask. The other was a tall but skinny man, wearing a black sports outfit.

The masked man thumped the sports guy with a smack, making him plummet to the ground. *Ouch! That was ruthless!* The sports guy got up courageously and tried to punch the masked man in the face. But, before he could, the masked man jumped and flipped to his back. Though it was impossible to see amid the dusky, desolate, and eerie atmosphere, the masked man could see perfectly. He could also perform astounding stunts. But, who was he? His identity remained unknown. Detectives were still trying to understand who he was and why he was fighting an innocent man.

The sports guy turned, about to punch, but the masked man put his hand up to halt the fist from touching him. The masked man somersaulted to reach behind the sports guy, giving him the worst scratch. He scratched him with four fingers, going from the bottom right to the top left of his face.

Bleeding heavily, the sports guy fell to his knees. Then, something unexpected occurred. Everything happened in the blink of an eye, within a millisecond. The masked man pointed at the sports guy with two fingers. Out of his fingers came black lightning, and struck the sports guy. The sports guy fell to the ground, unconscious.

The police arrived, and now the masked man was in big trouble. But, before the police could even land, the masked man managed an escape. He pulled out a sword and pointed it at a building. The sword shot towards the building and the handle released an attached rope. He then used it to swing out of the situation.

"If you have seen this masked man anywhere, take a picture, and send it to the Glazenia police for a reward of 100 bucks. If you capture the masked man, take him to the police for a reward of 200 bucks. This is Merla Karlin speaking," the newsagent in uniform spoke to us through the Holographic Television (HTV) as the video of the two men played on the side.

I watched the video with my mouth half-open. Many queries entered my mind. Who were these two people? Why were they fighting each other? How did lightning strike from the masked man's fingers? I kind of felt bad for the sports guy. Kind of. I liked the masked man. I don't know why, but I just did! I liked that cruel masked man who was attacking a normal person out for a walk. I might have gone crazy! Even after thinking of myself as crazy, I felt as if that cruel person was important to me.

"Kelly, Danica, it is time for you to sleep now. Good night," Mom said with her usual soft voice.

I reluctantly went to my bed and tried to sleep. I lay there, not able to snooze, my brain constantly going back to the masked man. After what seemed like decades, I fell asleep.

The next morning, I was woken up by Kelly's coughing. Kelly and I are identical twins. Like our mother, we are blue-eyed brunettes, with long, wavy hair and smooth rose-beige skin. However, Kelly is thin like our mother, and I am not.

I went downstairs for breakfast — cereal with milk. After I was done, I changed my clothes and tied my hair in a French braid.

After a while, Dad greeted us goodbye as he left for work. He is a tall and healthy red-haired man with dark brown eyes and freckles on his face. My younger, identical twin brothers take after him in features.

In a few minutes, I was ready to leave for school, but even before I could reach the garage, Mom came and told me to take my brother, Archie, along while Kelly took Andy. They are both seven years old. Speaking of my brothers, they were incredibly mischievous and difficult to handle when they were about three, not that they aren't now. They brought mud from the garden and sprinkled it all around the house. Then they turned the whole kitchen into a disaster zone with curd, chocolate, and many other food items. It was very hard to clean, but the twins helped by licking up all the chocolate and a little bit of the mud. Once, they flooded the entire washroom and living room, jumping on and splashing water all over the furniture and wetting everyone's feet. Besides, thanks to them, all the walls of our home are dyed with pens and crayons in various shapes and sizes of what appear to be monsters. One day, they went into hiding at night and fell asleep there. When Mom and Dad woke up the next morning — "Andy and Archie are missing!", "Where did they go?" — they were scared to death.

Once, the twins took out all the air from my football and crammed it with sand, which I realised only when I started practising some stunts, and it would barely move. One day, they took Kelly's favourite book and replaced it with some sort of paint gun, camouflaging it by making a fake book cover. When Kelly opened the book, she got badly sprayed by paint. When she went down for lunch, Mom shouted at the boys, Dad laughed, and I couldn't help but laugh a little too.

Anyways, I let Archie climb onto my Pegasus, Flake, a white stallion with wings. He hugged my waist so he wouldn't fall. I gave him a ride to school. When we landed, we got off and went our separate ways. Flake went back home.

I went into the school through the main gate and up to my class, 4G. First off, we had English, the most awful! All we did was write stories, paragraphs, or fake newspaper articles, or else we colour-coded figurative languages.

"First, everyone, write the date today. It's June 20, 13059," Miss Dazlina started. "Everyone done? Okay, so today, we will plan our own short stories. They have to be fictional. Can anyone remind me what fiction means? Let's see, Danica?"

"Who, me? Err… fiction is…" I was not good at English, alright. "Fiction is a book filled with fact-y stuff!"

"Incorrect. Kelly?"

"Fiction is a story not based on facts. Fictional stories can be myths, fantasy stories, etc.," Kelly said.

"Great job!" Miss Dazlina exclaimed. "So, as I was saying, today, we will plan our own fictional stories. They can be about anything we like. First, let's think of a mythical creature or an object that we'd like to add to our fictional stories. When you're done, raise your hand, and share with us what you have thought of."

I could be great at stuff like that. Making up unreal creatures or objects was my thing, though Kelly still topped every time. Kelly's hand shot through the air just five minutes after Miss had set the task.

"Kelly, would you like to tell the class about your creative idea?" Miss Dazlina said.

"Yeah, I created a pen. As soon as its ink touches a toy or any non-living thing, the thing comes alive," Kelly said.

I think her invention was better than a lollipop that could hypnotise someone. That was my invention, a lollipop. I, for the first time, had finished my work before Miss told us about the next task.

"Psst! Kelly! Do you mind drawing a lollipop for me?" I whispered to Kelly.

We had to draw a diagram, and she is better at it than I am. Thankfully, she said yes.

After our mythical creatures, we had to think of our main character. My character was pretty much just like me. Well, my character was me, except it was cooler and had superhuman abilities! In my story, Danica could fly and had a cyan and midnight blue cape.

After English, I had math, a brain dizzy-er. Math has all those weird questions.

"Today, we will focus on mental math. To do some brain warm-up, answer these questions," Miss Dazlina said.

Brain warm-up? I think it didn't just warm my brain; it melted it!

Miss asked us a few mental math questions and some over-enthusiastic students promptly answered.

"Great job! Okay, now answer the following questions in your notebook, but do it mentally. No calculating on paper."

I tried getting a fine look at Kelly's work. She had completed a lot of questions already. I quickly copied down all her answers.

The school continued to be boring.

Finally, when it was dispersal time, I dashed to Flake, who was waiting for me at the school parking and went back home. As soon as I reached home, I hopped on my bed to lie down. I had a lot of homework, but I would not do it now, hoping Kelly would do it for me. She would, like always. I would just need to pay her a few bucks, though.

When it was five in the evening, I went to the nearby park to meet my friends.

"Hi, guys!" I greeted my friends.

"What's up?"

"Sky." I chuckled.

"Let's go to the Air Stables and play something! I have brought my Pegasus," Trucia said.

I sat on my snow-white Pegasus and rode upwards. When we reached, in front of me lay an immense track made of firm clouds. I suggested we play Coltivyx.

"We haven't played Coltivyx for a long time. Do you mind repeating the rules?" Zenith asked as we started getting into the lanes.

"It's like horse riding," Trucia explained to Zenith. "Usually, Coltivyx includes weapons to fight off the opponent to make them fall off their Pegasus, which is dangerous. That is why we're not doing the real version. We just shoot paintballs at each other. So, just horse riding with Pegasus and paintball, okay?"

"1…" I said.

"2…" Mia said.

"3…" Trucia said.

"GO-lden chocolate!" Andy said.

Wait a second, Andy? Since when did he have a Pegasus? Plus, I didn't see him come.

"Andy, why are you on Kelly's Pegasus?" I asked.

"Because I wanted to come!" Andy replied.

"Who allowed you to?" I asked.

"Who cares about that?" Trucia said. "Now, GO!"

I zoomed off quickly. My Pegasus was quite hasty. I shot a paintball at Trucia because she was the trickiest to defeat and aimed right at her face, which slowed her down. I got to speed up. I was still third last out of the fifteen of us, Andy being seen only as a dot, miles behind us.

I was nearly hit by a paintball, but I ducked. Then, I stood up on my Pegasus, and as Flake galloped swiftly, I aimed my paintball at my friends. I targeted Trucia, but ended up shooting Max. Then, I aimed another one at Eleanor and got it spot-on.

A paintball was coming towards my feet, but I jumped right in time. By the time I sat back on Flake, I was very close to the finish line.

The good thing: Nobody had gone through the finish line yet.

The bad thing: Trucia and Eleanor were tied two meters away from the finish line.

"Faster, Flake!" I yelled.

He sped up a bit, but that didn't help. I aimed a paintball at Trucia. It was going to hit, but then she ducked. That distracted her just enough and slowed down her Pegasus.

I went ahead of Trucia and hit a paintball at Eleanor. She fell off her Pegasus and landed on the cloud track. I went ahead of her and… won!

"Danica! Danica! Can you even hear me? Come on. Let's go back home. We need to eat dinner and then — " I heard Kelly say from her friend's Pegasus on the far end.

"No way! I'm not studying. You can complete my homework for me," I said.

Homework was the most boring thing, and those was one of the few words you would never hear coming out of Kelly's mouth.

"I'm guessing you forgot a word. What do we call it again? Oh yeah, the *magic* word!" Kelly said sarcastically.

"Please," I said unwillingly.

Trucia started giggling about how desperately I had said "please" to my sister.

"Okay, now come home. Mom is calling. It's already eight o'clock," Kelly said.

"Fine. Bye, guys! See you tomorrow." I waved my friends goodbye and left on my Pegasus.

I landed in our Pegasus garage and walked towards the door. After ringing the doorbell, the white door opened in front of me. I went inside our two-storey house. There was a mammoth living room with the HTV against the wall on the right. A furry rug lay in front of the HTV, with a four-seater sofa behind it, a two-seater sofa on its left, and a pouffe on its right. Behind the living room was the stone dining room, or what I liked to call – the royal feast room. By royal feast, I mean that the dining table was so huge, it could fit a whole royal dinner! The fireplace was on the wall opposite the door, in the far corner. The kitchen was to the right of the dining table. It was vast, not quite a chef's dream, but extremely spacious. The stairs were right next to the main door.

The second storey had all the bedrooms. There were three walls, one to the right, one to the left, and one right in front. The left wall had two doors, the first leading to my bedroom and the second to Kelly's. On the front wall, there was only one door, to Mum and Dad's room. The right wall again had two doors leading to Andy and Archie's bedrooms.

My bedroom had a virtual gaming HTV. There was a dark blue bean bag sitting on the floor and beautiful LED lights on the ceiling borders that could turn into any colour I chose. The books in my room were either about animals or sports. The one I was currently reading was this great book about a famous roller-skater, Ember LeClair.

Kelly's room was more like a laboratory. It had a big, library-sized bookshelf with thousands of books. There was a big study table where Kelly studied, probably 24/7. She would normally burn the midnight oil studying and then sleep at three in the morning.

Mum and Dad's room was super neat, and I couldn't understand how that was possible. There wasn't much stuff in their room, though. They had a bed, a bedside table, a huge mirror, and cupboards.

Andy and Archie's rooms were completely identical, and I don't think they did it on purpose. The bed was cartoon themed (was it Batman?). If you opened any of their cupboards, a huge pile of junk would be come crashing down on you, which had happened to me once. Kelly had warned me, but I did it anyway. Their room also had high security. You couldn't even get past the door without a bucketful of water spilling on you. If you somehow survived that, there was slime, a slippery floor, paintballs, and more. They always kept adding something new!

There was a terrace on top. I often jumped off it using my gliders, which looked like webs made of cloth worn under both arms. Many times, I tried climbing down the house from the terrace using the rock-climbing wall Dad had installed.

I ate dinner quickly and went to my room. In there, I played video games for hours until Mum's usual weekend knock came, telling us it was time to sleep.

-2-
Sea Serpent

The next day, Mum told us that we were going to the water park. I had expected it to be an ordinary trip, nothing big.

We settled in our Phoenix 9000 flying car (a spherical vehicle with a flat bottom, having two windows and two doors). Whenever the car was flying, it had a blue holographic ring under it.

As we were riding through the city and peering down through the car windows, we could barely see any land cars or whatever you call them. There were probably one or two per mile and were quite old-fashioned. Normally, the sky was filled with flying cars, a few models being Phoenix — which was the latest — whilst the others were just Dragon and Unicorn or even Sphinx, Pegasus, etc. After ten minutes of soaring through the sky, we reached the water park.

"Okay, so where first?" I asked. "Mum, can Kelly and I go on our own? We've got our phones."

"Okay, darling. Just call us if you're lost and meet us at the Taco Tastes restaurant at two o'clock precisely. Now let's see, swimming costumes?"

"Yes, Mum."

"Map?"

"Yes, Mum."

"Towel?"

"We've got everything, Mum!" I said, annoyed.

"Okay, okay, take care. Also, come to Taco Tastes at two. Don't forget!"

So, we all split up.

"Hey, Danica, where to now?" Kelly asked.

"There is this water slide that drops vertically! Let's try it?" I suggested.

"Sure!"

We tried finding our way to the ride. When we reached, we saw a blue banner with the ride drawn on it and the name of the ride, Death Drop, written in bold. We looked around, trying to figure out what the ride looked like. There was a big pool in the middle and the base of a tube leading to it. After laying eyes on the ride, my heart nearly leaped out of my chest. There was a tower — 200 feet high — leading to the ride. It was the scariest ride of all time. I liked that.

"Ugh! Why do they make so many stairs!" Kelly said as we approached the last step.

"Let's get going. The slide seems interesting! Can I go first?" I asked.

"Yeah, okay," Kelly said, excitedly.

I went into the tube. It was almost vertical, with a flat floor stopping me from sliding down already. Like in a simulator, a voice said, "One… two... three…" and the floor slid open. The first 100 feet was a tunnel, then came a 100-foot-high drop with no tunnel this time. I screamed as loudly as possible, during the free fall, trying not to look down. The wind felt cold against my skin. When I landed, I created a huge splash, probably as tall as half the drop itself.

"Let's… do it again! Again," I said, breathing heavily after coming out of the ride.

We did it multiple times until we realised we had tried no other rides. So, we set off for another one, which was just two rides away. When we reached it, we saw a banner with a dark green crocodile with a human sitting on it. Crocville was written in bold blue text. We entered the green and blue-themed open area.

"What do you think this ride will be like? Can we stop for a drink? Oh, I'm shivering! Where's the towel? And what again is this ride —" I said, rapidly.

"Seriously! Will you calm down?" Kelly interrupted. "First things first; as you can see on the instruction board over here, for this ride, we will sit on fake crocodiles in that lake over there." She pointed at the lake in the middle. "Second, okay, let's stop for a drink. The water bottle should be here somewhere." Kelly passed me the bottle. "Here you go. Drink."

It made me feel way better.

"And finally, take this towel to cover yourself up," Kelly said while fetching my white towel and giving it to me.

"Okay yeah, I'm ready. Let's go for the ride!" I finally said after drinking water and wrapping myself with the towel for about five minutes.

So, we went and lined up in a short queue. In the blink of an eye, we found ourselves right at the front of a now quite long-looking queue. A person in a blue uniform helped us get onto those fake crocodiles safely. The hands of the crocodile were the handles, which we were supposed to use to steer, and there were seatbelts, of course, that we were required to wear.

Then, as soon as we received the signal, we started steering the crocodile all around, twisting it forward, backward, right, and left. We bumped into each other many times. The topmost speed was so fast that everything looked blurry, and it was hard to see anything properly. After about twenty minutes, we went towards the riverbank and out.

"That... was fine," Kelly said once we had come out.

"Yeah, not as good as I expected," I replied, full of amazement!

Then, we went to a coffee shop.

"I'd like two cups of hot chocolate, please," I told the waiter.

She went in and returned with a tray that had two cups of hot chocolate stationed on it. Kelly and I took our cups and started drinking.

The first sip I took made me say to myself, *'This hot chocolate has become cold! I don't think it is freshly made! I really wish this was hot.'*

I took another sip and my tongue burned just like it does when I eat the toast I make. The cup almost slipped out of my hand. I could not understand how that happened. At first, it was extremely shocking, but then, I remembered all the other times when something unusual and weird had happened.

When I was five, I needed water. Suddenly, I saw water floating towards me, and it went right into my mouth. There was one time when I touched a boiling mug, but it did not even burn my finger. Such things had started happening more and more.

So, I decided to tell someone, and Kelly was the perfect choice. She was quite smart and could figure stuff out. She was also the closest person to me.

"Hey, Kelly," I started, "do you know how my hot chocolate got hot suddenly when it was cold when we got it?" I felt weird saying this because it wasn't something big.

However, Kelly looked surprised. She grabbed my cup to check for herself. "How on earth did that happen? The wind is completely cold today. How is that possible? I'll search for my books when we reach home."

I was taken aback. I didn't realise that Kelly would think of it as a big deal. I was expecting a reply like this, *'It's probably nothing, just a cup of cold chocolate getting heated suddenly.'*

When we were done with our hot chocolate, it was already 2 p.m.; so we headed to Taco Tastes as Mum had instructed. When we reached there, we saw our parents sitting with our brothers at a six-seater table. Kelly and I sat down next to our parents.

"So, where did you go?" Mom asked us while we were eating some delicious red sauce cheesy pasta and noodles. *Yum!*

"We went to Death Drop, a 200-foot-high vertical drop, and then to Crocville, where we sat on fake crocodiles. After that, we went to Teacups Café for hot chocolate and —" I was going to say how my cup got hot suddenly but then I decided not to, "— and yeah." Changing the subject, I said, "Mum, look!"

"Yes?" she replied.

"That ride looks amazing. Can we please go there?" I said.

"Which one?" Mum asked.

"That one!" We both said together, pointing at the ride with a red rollercoaster drawn on a blue banner.

"Sure! Why not?" Mum said.

We all went in. The ride was a huge rollercoaster that had glass walls and a ceiling to cover as it went underwater! We, as a whole family, took a compartment for ourselves and wore our seatbelts.

Then, it all happened, really quickly. We sped downwards, then went upwards slowly, looping once, twice, and a third time. We plunged downwards so fast that everything around us became a blur. Suddenly, the ride slowed as we went underwater, revealing an amazing sight of the underwater pool.

It had beautiful underwater plants like kelps, muskgrass, and some coral reefs. There were many fishes and breathtaking creatures around. The killer whale swam around calmly. The blue whale was showing off its enormous size. The starfish sat on the bottom while the oysters were keeping their pearls safe. The goldfish tried to hide in a coral reef with the bluefish. The zebrafish, the rainbow trout, the mandarin fish, the butterflyfish, and the clownfish, all swam around in schools or alone. The sea turtles were roaming at the bottom of the pool in slow motion.

There were a thousand more varieties of fish! Kelly was easily able to identify all of them, while I sat confused wondering which was which.

We were so absorbed in the scene underwater that we did not notice we were going back upwards after a big underwater loop. As we reached the outer surface of the sea, the roller coaster started zooming twice as quickly as before. We did another loop and then were taken down into the sea.

Inside the sea, there were beautiful fishes once again. This time, even Kelly couldn't guess some of them. We also spotted jellyfish and an octopus. Then, we saw a shark — a huge one swimming around, hunting for food. But, of course, since there was glass, we had nothing to worry about. The shark was zooming towards us, faster and faster; it got closer.

"Kelly, what's that fish over there?" I asked, pointing at a rainbow-coloured fish.

She replied with bubbles.

"Come on, can you stop making bubbles!"

But then, I noticed that there was no glass around us! We had been so much absorbed in looking at the shark that we did not notice the glass coming off!

Why wasn't Kelly able to speak but I was? How was I able to breathe? Then, when I turned to look at the shark, which was coming closer to us, and saw the people on the ride breathless, I decided that those questions could be thought of later. I knew one thing for sure; I needed to save the lot myself because I was the only one who could breathe underwater at that point of time.

But, how was I, an ordinary nine-year-old, supposed to save all these people from a shark? At that thought, my heartbeat started speeding up. My legs trembled. My hair started standing tall. The shark's yellow eyes gazed at me with a wicked look.

I could not think of any way to escape out of the situation. Kelly was the smarter one among both of us. But, here I was the one who needed to think quickly and act fast… I kept saying to myself, *I need to save them! I need to save them!*

Then, somehow, a giant bubble surrounded everyone on the roller coaster, except me. Besides, now everyone was able to breathe, which meant they were safe. However, I wasn't.

I knew that I was the one who had to defeat the shark, and probably, no miracle could help me this time. But, how was I supposed to defeat it?

The dark grey shark was now closer than ever, probably just one metre away. I thought in my mind, *This is going to chop me in half; if only I could fight it!* As I said that in my mind, I expected something to happen, something miraculous, just like in other situations. But, all that happened was the shark was opening its mouth wide.

Then, I saw a tall stick made of ice that I hadn't seen before. I quickly ran towards it and grabbed it. I used it to stab the shark, but I looked dumb as it didn't even scratch. Then, suddenly, the shark closed its wide mouth, clenched its teeth, and tried to bite me. I swam as fast as I could, zooming all around, trying to get away from it, but soon realised that it wouldn't get tired unlike me, who was losing all strength.

I kept increasing the amount of power I was exerting to hit the shark. At one point, I stabbed it quite hard. It fell back and couldn't move. I went a little closer and then a little more. That was my biggest mistake. When I was right next to the shark, I raised the stick, about to stab it, until something pushed me back harder than I could resist. I fell onto the bubble and bounced off. *Ouch!*

What I saw as soon as I regained my focus was a humongous sea animal in front of me. Its yellow eyes with green outlines and black, oval pupils gave me a 'tasty-meal-for-today' look. Its serpent tongue was ready to devour me. The body of the creature looked like a long, green snake. It had yellow spikes on its back that looked sharper than the venomous fangs it was going to eat me with. I recognised it to be a sea serpent. I also recognised that there was no way I was beating a sea serpent and a shark both together, not that I would have been able to defeat a sea serpent alone.

I looked at the ice stick in my hand. I noticed that one of the flat sides was now sharp and pointy. *How on earth did that happen?* I then realised that there was no time to think of such minor things because the sea serpent was raging upon me.

The sea serpent leapt to grab me. I cowered. The beast's eyes made me shudder. When I managed to tap into the brave side of me, I jumped up and landed on the sea serpent's back. It was shaking its head, trying to get me off itself, but I had dug my fingers into its rough scales tight enough to stay on it.

The shark started swimming away, scared that the sea serpent would grab it. So now, I just had to fight the most dangerous animal in the whole sea, great!

I tried to poke the sea serpent with the sharper side of the stick, but I just ended up making a fool of myself, again. I stayed on its back, making sure to keep a tight grip. I tried pulling it backwards, stabbing, poking, and kicking it, but none made any difference to the huge sea serpent.

I finally poked the beast in the eye. It let out an ear-piercing shriek of pain, slicing through my ears. With the sea serpent blind now, it was a bit easier to defeat it, a bit. It still had a great sense of hearing and could listen to even the softest sound.

I jumped off the sea serpent's back and went back to the ground, so I could fight it better. I stabbed it in the back once more, and this time the stick went through its body. Blood trickling, the giant turned around and swung its tail towards the sound of me swimming. The tail slammed hard, pushing me towards the shield protecting thirty people on the roller coaster. I hit it and rebounded once more. I had a big bruise on my back that was unbearably painful.

That tail's hit drained away all the strength that I had. I couldn't resist the pain anymore. Even though I was weak, I still tried my best to make absolutely no sound, so it couldn't hear me. I realised that if the beast would have no sense of hearing and sight, it would not be able to locate me and everyone else.

Though my back hurt badly, I wasn't in immense pain anymore. Actually, it had stopped hurting and was back to normal again. Believe me, I was as clueless as you are about how that happened!

Anyway, back to the defeating-the-sea-monster part. I decided to hit its ear. So, I made some noise, this time on purpose, and it leapt down towards me. I promptly jumped up and, like before, landed on the back of the sea serpent.

With a little shaky grip, I grabbed the ice sword with my right hand and stabbed its right ear successfully. It roared as a surge of pain sliced through its body. It started shaking, and despite my tightest grip, I fell down.

I tried swimming back onto its back, but this time it wasn't foolish enough to let me. It knew that I wanted its hearing and sight senses to wear off. The sea serpent, or as I would like to call it, Spikey, was trying to stab me with its enormous tail. Since it couldn't hear as efficiently as it used to, it ended up wagging its tail on the opposite side from where I was treading water.

I realised that I could get on Spikey's back when it was looking the other way. So, I waited for the right moment to jump, and that was when its tail was pointing at me. I jumped forward and sat on it. I hastily stabbed the left ear, making its sense of hearing wear off.

Now, I could get everyone out of the water and back to safety. But, how? I did not know that. Just as I started going towards the bubble, Spikey's tail again pushed me away, stabbing me even more badly this time. My stomach hurt severely; I could barely move. How did it locate me this time?

I then remembered that I had seen a YouTube video about sea serpents and their senses. With the help of their spikes, they could feel everything inside the sea without sight or hearing abilities because of the vibrations, waves and bubbles. It was going to be nearly impossible for me to beat Spikey now!

I panicked so much, I couldn't even think properly (not that I could in normal situations, either). My mind was a blank, dark, empty room with nothing but fear.

Suddenly, I got a weird feeling, as if I was being pulled into a black hole. Everything was turning black. After that, I don't remember a thing that happened.

"Danica! Danica! Wake up. Are you alright? Mum, Danica isn't waking up."

I woke up with a start as I faintly heard Kelly's voice. She sounded so worried.

"W…what happened? Why are we here? How did we escape?" I asked. My mind was blank.

"Oh phew! Mum, she's alright," Kelly reassured Mum, whose face was right above me.

"Oh darling, how are you feeling? Are you alright?" Mum said, sounding even more worried than Kelly.

She hugged me, patting me on my back. I felt droplets fall onto my hair, which were probably Mum's tears.

"Yeah, I'm fine. But, what happened exactly? Like, I got a weird feeling, and then everything was just blank," I said, now even more confused as I said it aloud.

"You suddenly started acting like a superhero. You first took a rope that was basically water, sort of like jelly. You tied the rope around the sea monster. Somehow, it was easily tied into the shape of a ball. Then you came straight to us, lifted the bubble as if it were a football, and ran across the surface of the ocean to a nearby island. As soon as you landed, you fell on your back and lost consciousness," Kelly spoke in a single breath, as surprised as I was.

"Now rest, both of you. I'll be sitting right here, making sure you're safe, okay?" Mum said in her usual polite way.

"Okay, Mum, good night," I said completely exhausted. "I mean good evening-night!"

"That doesn't make any sense. Now, let's sleep, I'm tired," Kelly said.

"Where exactly are we?" I asked.

"We're on the Southern Isle," Kelly said, but she looked as if we were in a spooky tent on Halloween. "Uh-oh! It's one of the four Enchanted Isles, which means it is enchanted!"

I laughed at that one. *It was a nice way to spook me out, but sis, you got to try better than that!*

"There are no such things as enchantments, silly!" I said, still laughing at her joke.

"I'm serious. Don't you pay attention in class? We learned about it just this Tuesday," Kelly said, now looking even more spooked up.

"Now don't go on lecturing me about focusing in class, Mom!" I said sarcastically.

Kelly always tells me to organise my stuff, clean up my bedroom, study for end-of-the-year assessments, finish homework, focus in class, and take notes of what we learn. She even made a daily schedule for me. She acts like my mother.

I suddenly realised that it wasn't only me, my sister, and Mum on this island. There were many people. They were the people who were on the rollercoaster ride. All of them looked thirsty and hungry, besides being exhausted... *What if this place is enchanted, then what will we do? Maybe only the forest is enchanted.*

I decided I to go and help them. I would make a large border around them so that they don't go out of it. But how? How exactly was I supposed to make such a huge border to fit thirty people, allowing only Kelly and me to go in and out of the border?

Instantly, my thought was answered. A ginormous water semi-bubble came out of the sea and floated towards everyone. It landed right around them and stayed. I was amazed. How did that happen? It was like the waves just responded to me. Though how was I supposed to enter the barrier?

I tried walking in, and I went through. Kelly did the same, and she went through it too, though that made me a bit worried. If Kelly could go through, and so could I, then this barrier would let other things and people through, even enchantments. Then this barrier would be useless! An idea suddenly popped into my head.

"Dad, can you check if you can get out of the bubble?" I asked.

He went forward and tried going through the bubble but bounced back. So, this meant that only Kelly and I could go out and come back in. Great! I then went into the middle of the bubble and made an announcement.

"Okay, guys, so this bubble is to ensure that you all are safe. No one can come in or go out of this bubble except Kelly and me. Err... I will go and fetch some big leaves so that you can sleep on them and relax. I will also go every day to get food and water for everyone. We will be staying here for a while till we come up with a plan to get ourselves out of this mess. Make yourself comfortable. Thank you," I said.

I turned around to leave, but then Mum stopped me.

"Where do you think you're going?" she said, her hands on her hips

I turned around to look at her. “Well, someone’s going to have to get food and water, and since I’m the only one who can get out of the bubble, I’ll go!”

“Ahem, Ahem!” Kelly said.

I rolled my eyes. “I mean Kelly and I are the only ones who can go out of the bubble.”

“I am not letting you go out of this border! Do you understand me?” Mum said.

It is so annoying when she doesn’t allow me to do something that is too dangerous. Even Kelly disagreed with Mum. She wanted to go too. We reluctantly went onto the sand, looked at all the tired faces sadly, and went to sleep.

I had a dream. I saw myself, or someone who looked like me, in a dark and misty forest, pointing at a big tree — the only dead tree in the whole forest. I saw her climb the tree.

I would have seen more, but then Kelly had to wake me up! Couldn’t it wait for a little longer? No, I suppose it couldn’t.

-3-

Southern Isle

"Wake up! Wake up! Do you want to go and get food or not?" Kelly whispered. "I know Mum hasn't allowed us but just come on, let's go!"

'No way, she didn't! Did she just disobey what Mum said? This is probably the first time she did so! Are my ears playing tricks on me?'

"Could you repeat what you said? I think I heard you wrong, I heard you say that you want to disobey Mum! Hehe, my ears might not be working toda—"

"No, you heard me right. Now are you coming or not? We've not got much time," she said.

We quickly went out of the bubble, took a deep breath, and lunged into the forest.

The forest gave me a chill down my spine. My stomach prickled. A dark, misty forest was the last on my bucket list. The trees were so tall, with brown, dead leaves, and the mist fogging the happy thoughts I had thought of just this morning. As we walked in deeper, I felt a tingle in my stomach. I was shivering, even though the forest wasn't cold.

There was this feeling that we were being followed, but I thought of it as the fog misting my thoughts. I felt sick already.

I was missing the bubble we had been peacefully sleeping in. Speaking of sleeping, I remembered that my lookalike in my dream had shown me something in a forest like this. What if this was the forest in my dream? Even if it was, I was not in the mood of thinking about that right now, so I just kept walking.

After a few minutes, Kelly did the most useless thing. She went towards a thin sheet of tree bark and took my ice stick, the one I used to battle the sea serpent.

"Kelly, it's not the time to draw!" I said, annoyed by her habit of drawing anytime she found a sheet of paper or drawing material.

"It is, it's the only way I don't get chills down my spine, the only way I can relax a bit and think properly," she replied.

I got so annoyed by her concept that drawing kept her relaxed. Whenever I tried to draw (which was almost never), I would get agitated and shout at anyone who dared to talk to me.

She drew a big buffet. I think she was hungry too. Looking at the drawing, my stomach growled. Then I heard another growl, which was much louder. It couldn't have been my stomach this time. But, if it wasn't my stomach, then... my question was answered right there, right then.

A tiger that looked like it was on fire, entered the narrow space we had been roaming and stood in front of us. The predator gazed at us with a scowl. It made a short roar, enough to scare anyone into freeze mode rather than flight-or-fight response. I instantly recognised it to be a Fotigris.

The burning Fotigris first moved towards Kelly. Just as it took off a leap, I ran towards Kelly, defenceless, and came in between the Fotigris and her. I was expecting to be burned, to be on fire, and turned to ashes, but nothing happened. I mean nothing except the fact that I screamed for no reason.

The fire from the Fotigris did no harm to me. When it was a millimetre away from me, the fire turned into smoke. It was as if I had a millimetre-thick layer of water covering me. I did not know how it happened, though questions were flooding my mind. *How am I not burned? How did the fire turn to smoke just as it was about to touch me? How on earth am I alive? What is so extraordinary in me that these miracles are happening? Or is it just the Fotigris that has a fire that is incapable of burning people?* All these questions tried overtaking my mind, making me forget that I was in the middle of a dark forest, fighting a Fotigris.

I tried forcing my thoughts to align with the fact that I was in a forest. When I did come back to my senses, I still had the curious questions in the back of my mind, which I wished would leave my mind and come back when I needed them to.

Kelly had already finished five drawings by the time I came back to the real world. The first one was a buffet. The second one was a long and sharp diamond-shaped sword. The third one was a big bucket and many cups. The fourth one was a map of the forest. The fifth one was the best of them all — thirty mattresses. She is so good at drawing; it was as if she were born with the skill.

After Kelly did her drawings, she said she was way more in the mood for fighting, so she stood up. It was quite weird how she, in the middle of the forest, started drawing all those weird things! But, she did fight better now.

The Fotigris came raging towards me, about to burn me again, but Kelly splashed water onto the Fotigris. The Fotigris now looked like an ordinary tiger, but it seemed to have gotten weak. It took a few steps back, stumbled, fell onto the ground, and died. Kelly and I rushed away.

Kelly still had her drawings with her, but one of the five wooden sheets was blank.

"What happened to that drawing of yours? Where did it go?" I asked her.

"I don't know how, but the bucket I drew came alive! My art teacher always told me to draw whenever I needed something, but only to draw the thing that I needed the most. So, I drew all the stuff we really needed and the bucket came alive somehow!" she replied.

Now, that is why she, out of nowhere, started sketching on that thin sheet of bark. I had more questions I was itching to ask.

"By the way, do you know how I didn't get burned when the Fotigris almost set me on fire? Do you know why the flames that were about to touch me just turned to smoke?" I burst into questions.

But, I only got a one-word reply. "Dunno."

Kelly looked a bit confused. I then remembered what happened with the sea serpent and had a lot of curiosity about that as well.

"And, why did the ice stick suddenly appear out of nowhere when I was fighting the sea serpent? Why did a bubble come around you and the others, but not me? Why did I not remember how I had escaped from the sea serpent, and as you had told me, I was running on the water, right? How did I do that?" I asked.

I got no different answer than the other one.

"Dunno," Kelly repeated.

We walked on. This time, I was not at all scared for some reason, maybe because I was still thinking about how the miracles that happened to me, happened. Or maybe because I felt like I could defeat anything if I could defeat a burning tiger.

As we were moving forward, I saw a small ray of light shining through the mist, from far away. I started jogging towards the source. The closer I got, the better I felt, as if I was running towards food, which at that time would have felt like a diamond.

When I reached, I saw piles of fruits lying on the ground, as if fruits had been falling down the tree for years and no one came to take them. I wanted to take a humongous pile of these fruits back to the bubble, probably a four-foot-tall and a two-foot-wide bucketful of fruits.

Bucketful. Oh yeah, I could use the bucket that Kelly had drawn, to take the fruits back to the bubble. But, where is the bucket?

"Kelly, do you know where the bucket is? I think we could fill these fruits in it," I said.

"Good idea, but... Uh-oh! I think I left the bucket back where we assassinated the tiger. Let's go and get it quickly. I think the sun is coming up now," Kelly said.

I nodded in agreement. We both took fruits for ourselves and ran back towards the tiger.

When we reached, we saw a big surprise waiting for us. By big, I mean big.

"But, he died right in front of us! How is it possible that he is alive?" I said, whining. I felt quite tired, my legs felt numb, and I barely had the ability to stand.

The tiger was completely awake, but it was not on fire this time.

"The tiger's a she, not he, silly! Didn't you see the rectangle footprints? Males have square footprints. You're so bad at gender recognition. And, she'd fainted, not died," Kelly replied, sarcastically.

That was the most annoying thing by her! As if I would think about what the shape of the footprints was.

Suddenly, I noticed a white glint. As I turned to look at it, the glow disappeared, leaving a thin, long diamond-shaped sword with pointed corners on the two sides. There were sheets of wood under the sword, two of them were blank. It was the sword Kelly drew that came alive! The Fotigris raced towards the sword. I ran faster than I ever did! The Fotigris ran even faster and grabbed the sword in her mouth. I ran towards the tiger, trying to snatch the sword from her mouth, but the grip was too tight.

I saw branches on the tree behind me, but it was too high for me to reach. The tree was long and thin, so I could easily hug it.

I decided to climb the tree using the climbing skills I had learned from my karate teacher. I went towards the tree and hugged it. I got a tight grip on the tree with my arms, and then I folded my legs around it. I moved my hands a little upwards and pulled my legs up, continuing this until I reached close to the vines. Next, I gripped it even more tightly, now being twelve feet above the ground. I slowly let go of one hand and grabbed a branch quickly.

I could use the branch to poke the tiger, then the tiger would roar, letting the sword fall to the ground for me to take. Of course, now that I think about it, my plan probably had a 0.0000000001% chance of working.

I had never climbed this high before. Kelly was still trying to distract the tiger, dodging her whenever she attacked. I hesitated. I was about to climb down, but the tree had started bending to my side. I felt like I was about to fall, but then I realised that the tree had bent so much that I could easily get off it and not get hurt. I tried leaping off. I put one foot to the ground, but then, the tree recoiled and went to the opposite side, taking me with it. It kept swaying from side to side, and soon, I lost my grip. As I was falling, tears rolled down my face, and the wind rushed through me.

I would have broken my bones, but didn't. I had landed onto a soft mattress. One of the mattresses Kelly drew! It came alive. I owe Kelly a lifetime; if it weren't for her, I would be dead.

Now wasn't the time to think of this; I still had a tiger — who had started wiping her fangs and taken out the sword from her mouth, preparing for the treat (me) lying on the mattress — to defeat.

I fell onto a mattress, yes. I fell from twelve feet, smashing face-first onto a mattress. My face turned cherry red, and my whole body followed suit. My stomach started to hurt terribly. If I bent my back even slightly, it would burn more than fire, though I didn't know how fire burns felt. Overall, Kelly just saved me from dying but not from experiencing excruciating pain throughout my body. Nonetheless, if I didn't get up quickly, it wouldn't make a difference if the mattress saved me or not; I would be eaten by the tiger.

I bent my back a little, so I could get up, and *CRACK!* My back cracked. I stood up normally, trying to bear the pain. I quickly grabbed the sword that was lying on the floor and started stabbing the tiger hard, but she wouldn't get hurt.

Then, suddenly, the tiger jumped onto me. I tumbled to the ground, screaming loudly. How loud do you think I screamed? Amplify it 100 times. Kelly tried hitting and kicking the tiger, but it did no good. The tiger poked a sharp claw into my thigh. Blood dripped down. Tears flowed down my face. The soreness was unbearable, and pain stung my body. My grip loosened, and I let go of the sword.

All of a sudden, the tiger just fell down. There was blood on her back. Kelly had used the sword and stabbed her.

I had gone through enough stuff today; all I wanted to do was rest, sleep for an entire day and night, and wake up the day after tomorrow. At that point, getting food was on my top-five list, and going to the bubble was at number one on the list.

The tiger, dead, would not disturb us anymore, thankfully. We quickly grabbed the immense bucket and ran towards the fruit tree, which I was truly reluctant ; I had had enough for the day.

I suddenly realised that it was morning, which meant Mum was awake. *Uh-oh!*

I couldn't even run because of the bite, so I had to walk. Even that was difficult to do. I started hopping on one foot. I told Kelly to run to the tree, and that I would try walking as fast as I could. She did that and ran with great speed; I wished I could do that.

The blood had started drying, and the pain began to lessen. When I saw a lake, I felt a strong urge to go and just dip my legs in. I sat on the ground and put my legs into the water. It felt so soothing, and relaxing. I felt like I was never bitten. But then, something happened that made the lake very unrelaxing.

I got stung, badly. On a closer look, I found that it was a jellyfish. Being stung by a jellyfish was worse than a tiger's bite. I got stung on my good leg, the leg that didn't get bitten. I fell backwards and felt paralysed. I could see and hear everything that was going on around me, but I couldn't move.

What felt like ten years later, Kelly came and examined my whole body after she managed to take my leg out of the lake. She noticed the jellyfish sting on my leg and poured something on it. It reduced the pain, and I was able to move.

I put my leg again in the lake. I know it sounds crazy, but I needed the calm sensation to get my sting to heal. When I saw that my leg felt better, I quickly took it out so I wouldn't get stung again. When I stood up and started walking, I realised I could walk easily; the tiger bite wasn't hurting. I checked and saw a permanent scar.

Kelly had gathered the whole bucketful of fruits by then. So, we started going back to the bubble. For the rest of the time, we didn't encounter anything wild, just a fierce wind rushing by. We ran at our topmost speed, even with the heavy bucket in our hands.

When we reached the bubble, I said to myself, "Home Sweet Home," even though it wasn't our home.

I entered the bubble and wished that I hadn't.

"You still went? You disobeyed me? I was worried sick! You could have been killed," Mum shouted at the top of her voice.

"We had to do something, being the only ones who can get out of the bubble," I urged.

"What exactly happened out there? I need the truth. Even if you have gotten hurt, I need to know," Mum said.

"Well, err… we… might have encountered a Fotigris, but

then we put her out of fire —" I said, wishing I hadn't, because Mum looked like she was scared, very scared.

"Then we went to get fruits from a tree but forgot the bucket where the Fotigris was —" Kelly continued.

"When we reached, the Fotigris looked like a normal tiger. We started fighting it. It might have poked me with its claw."

It looked like Mum would go crazy right here, and she did go crazy.

"It did what? Show me!" Mum said.

I reluctantly showed her the scar on my right leg.

"Does it hurt? Let me see how I can make it better," Mum said, even more anxious, tears dripping down her eyes.

I knew I shouldn't have told her.

"It doesn't hurt, Mom. In fact, I feel like it never happened," I said, trying to calm her down. It partially worked.

"And, then we went to put fruits in the bucket and came back here," I said, not willing to tell Mum about the jellyfish sting.

"Oh dear, I should have stayed awake to watch you guys," Mum said. "Don't go off again, you understand?"

I decided to do so, but I didn't know how else we would get food. On second thought, I just realised how we could get food. *Draw only what you need.*

"Kelly, we won't need to go out of the bubble ever again. You can simply 'draw only what you need,' which, in this case, is food," I suggested.

"Good idea."

She started drawing already.

Suddenly, a glow of light came into the bubble, and we saw a huge buffet! I think that was the buffet Kelly had drawn in the forest!

I went to the middle of the bubble and announced, "Eat up, everybody! There is water and food. Fill your stomach until you can't eat more."

Everybody ran towards the buffet, picked their plates, and piled a variety of dishes on them. They started eating hot food — french fries, spaghetti, pasta, pizza, sandwiches, noodles, soup, waffles, cakes, pancakes, doughnuts — the food you would never expect to appear in the middle of the forest.

I grabbed a doughnut and started munching on it. I was so hungry. As soon as I ate the first bite, I felt so good, it was like an energy booster. Then I took a plate and filled it with many delicious dishes. Later, I drank some litchi and mango milkshake.

Once I had eaten enough, I felt sleepy, I put the mattress that had appeared in the middle of the forest onto the ground and slept. And, I dreamt again, continuing from where I had left.

My lookalike went into a tree and ended up in a wide room, perhaps a secret hideout.

Then my dream changed.

There were millions of people, battling millions of people.

I woke up with a start. It was the next day. Whoa! I slept for a whole day. When I woke up, I felt more relaxed. For a few seconds, I felt like I was at home, but then I realised I wasn't. My head felt clearer; I felt more active; it was as if I had never gone into the forest in the first place, which meant I had a good sleep. I got to my feet and had my breakfast. Kelly had "cooked" (drawn) some pancakes, waffles, milk, fruits, and cornflakes. My mouth-watering, I quickly feasted on the food.

Next, I wanted to do something active. I went to the seashore and swam there. I dived in, able to breathe and talk, not at all wet. I did a few frontflips and backflips, and then, I lay down on the surface of the sea. After that, I called Kelly in.

We played a game of sharks and fish. I was the shark and Kelly the fish. I tried catching her. Kelly was doggy paddling, trying to get away from me. She wasn't so good at swimming. I caught her by the leg. This time, Kelly was the shark. I kept dodging her attacks, and swimming away every time she was within a metre from me. We could have taken a million millenniums, but I suppose we couldn't live that long.

Then, something happened. There was a loud bang inside the bubble. Someone was banging the bubble so hard, it could have broken. It took only a few minutes to realise that the 'someone' was my mum! I suppose we did go out of the bubble, but what could happen in a sea with no fish or dangerous creatures? Did I say no dangerous creatures?

Think again, Danica! You got stung by a jellyfish in a small lake that seemed so soothing at first. How could you think that the sea around an enchanted island was not dangerous?

Anyways, as I expected, or did not expect, a giant creature came to us. The creature looked like the sea serpent, except for the fact that it had nine heads. A hydra! The problem with it having nine heads was that five of those heads were facing me, and four were facing Kelly. Believe me, you do not want to see the mouth of a hydra. Its humongous fangs looked like big blades in an armoury with green gooey and slimy venom!

It all was extremely disgusting and yucky! The blood-curdling eyes were looking right into mine. The face was especially daunting! My fists were clenched in fright under the water.

Looking at the scene, Mum fell to the ground, weeping, feeling helpless. I suppose the barrier was a good thing, Mum couldn't get herself into dangers like these.

Suddenly, I noticed a sword appear in my hand, a sword made of ice. I didn't think I had the courage to fight a humongous nine-headed sea serpent, the single-headed sea serpent was bad enough! Even though it was a life-or-death situation, I had fight or die, and of course, I was going to fight!

I still hesitated, but not having much time, I slashed the sword at one of the necks of the hydra. Only then I realised the big mistake I had made. I remembered what it said in the hydra book I read a long time ago, probably four weeks ago. The hydra grew two heads because I slashed one with a sword!

I knew I had no choice but to run. I was quite far from the bank of the sea, which meant it would be harder for me to escape. I gulped. My throat had a sore-feeling inside. My hands shivered with fright. My legs had become jelly, trying to lift my weight. I knew it! I knew the time had come. It was bound to happen someday. After all the dangers I had been through, I knew this day would come. This was the end. At the thought of it, butterflies started flying in my stomach and head. I felt like I would faint right there, but again, I wouldn't be alive much longer to faint. The hydra had already opened its mouth, ready to chop me in half for its dinner.

I had experienced the same weird feeling when I saw the sea serpent. But, unlike my incident with the sea serpent, I could remember what happened after that. I suddenly started controlling the hydra. I moved my hand to the right, and the hydra's heads banged to the right; then I moved my hand to the left, and the hydra's heads banged to the left. I kept doing that from side to side until the hydra got tired.

At first, it looked like the hydra was going away, but it turned to swing its tail onto me. The hydra pushed me far, but sadly, it wasn't onto land, it was even farther than land, into the water again.

Normally, I would seek for sea and water because that's where I felt relaxed, but this was not a normal situation. I swam fast, not towards land, but towards the hydra. I was not a selfish human who would just leave her sister behind.

When I went back to the hydra, I saw that Kelly was just drawing. The hydra, right in front, was wondering why Kelly didn't even care to fight for her life. Then, I noticed she was drawing on the surface of the sea and the sketch was being etched on the water. How could that happen? After she was done etching, she sort of just swiped through her sketch and it came alive. Where did she learn that from? The thing she drew turned out to be a useless circular disk; no actually, two circular disks. Kelly passed me one of the disks, and I somehow understood what she was trying to do. I caught the disk and stood on it.

I knew the hydra was almost about to eat me, but I tried not to think about it. The disk started hovering, with me on it. A hoverboard! I steered the hoverboard to move forward. The hydra tried its best to bite me. It ripped my shirt but missed biting me. The hoverboard wasn't very fast, that's why I had to dodge, at least twenty times, evading each of the hydra's heads coming down at me.

A head came towards me, and I ducked. Another one was about to attack me when I jumped and landed on the head of the hydra. The hoverboard was now two metres away from the head that I was standing on. I made a jump but ended up falling into the sea, from a height of twenty metres.

Somehow, I didn't touch the sea. Instead, I found myself holding the hoverboard. I pulled myself up and continued riding. Soon, I realised that I was far from the hydra. Quite far. I jumped out of the hoverboard, creating a big splash, and swam back to the bank of the sea.

I got out and ran to the bubble. I was somehow dry, but Kelly was not. She was soaking wet.

When I was in, I expected a huge lecture from Mum, but instead, she said, "Are you two alright? Did you get hurt? You two looked like heroines out there!"

Mum looked pleasantly surprised by what we had done there. She hugged us both tightly.

"No, Mom, we're fine!" We both said, happy that Mum just called us heroines.

She had said it a couple of times, but this time I knew she wasn't just trying to make us feel good, instead, she was telling us what she truly felt.

"Now promise me, you will not take a step out of this bubble. Not a single step," Mum said.

"We promise," Kelly and I said together.

Mom managed a smile.

My legs hurt after all that fighting. I went straight to the mattress and jumped onto it. I didn't dream at all this time.

-4-

Dark World

I heard footsteps, this time for real, not in a dream. I suddenly woke up. When I did, I figured out the mess I had put myself into. I saw myself in a metallic room. The room was big enough for me to lie down but its ceiling was too low for me to stand. There was no water, no food, nothing. There didn't even seem to be a door. The only thing there was, was me.

I tried to sleep, but I just couldn't, the metal hurt my bones. Who even put me here in the first place? I could taste evil. Cold and harshness went through my nostrils. All I could feel was the metal squishing my bones. I suddenly heard a voice, a cold male voice.

"Well, hello there, my fine guest, please do make yourself at home. This is a home that, I thought, would be better for you than a rusty mattress inside a weird bubble barrier thing," he said. He sounded evil, and he crackled a lot.

"How did you manage to enter?"

"I didn't come in, but I had one of my men come and get you. Just a little potion trick of mine. So, if you're comfortable, can you tell me why, my teammate, you were having an awful time? Did Edward tell you to come to the Island? Ooh! Is that you, Alice? My spirit says hi!"

Alice? Edward? Teammate? What does it all mean?

"Who are Alice and Edward, and how come I am your teammate? What are you talking about?" I demanded.

"Master Ed hasn't told you anything? Oh, dear! Well, it is better for me if you don't know. The lesser you know the better! Any questions? Don't ask," he said and left the mic.

"Wait! Come back!"

Too late, he had already left.

Now what? My throat was sore, and my back and bones were hurting. My stomach was in knots. Butterflies were twirling around my head. I was seeing things through a blurry barrier.

All I wanted to do was sleep, but I couldn't. My mind was racing. Who was that guy? How was I going to leave that ridiculous place? No idea. There was nothing in here that I could use to rescue myself. I was a prisoner for life. I preferred the hydra better, where I was in the sea with my sister to back me up. Here, I had no one and nothing. Speaking of my sister, I really hoped Kelly was alright. She might have been captured as well. My eyes couldn't stay open for long. Soon enough, I fell asleep.

I woke up with a start when I heard a voice outside the room. It must have been a guard or something.

I tried to hear or sense something, anything. Then I realised that I was able to breathe. *Where is the air coming from?* I scanned the place and saw a hole in the ceiling. I put my finger through the hole to find something. Only then did I realise, the room was made of wood. It was painted silver to make me think it was metal, so I wouldn't try breaking it apart. I had a black belt in karate, and it was easy for me to break the roof. Soon, I was out of the cage I had been trapped in for hours.

I heard a siren wailing from a distance. Maybe they could help me. But then, I heard footsteps coming towards me. Guards! Guards were swarming all around the box. Can't the surprises rest? Nope.

Coming out of the box was a big mistake.

Guards were all around. Faces were staring at me. Grim faces. Gloomy faces. Stern faces. Each of them was wearing black clothes. They had long jet-black blades.

I decided to run. Though, that wouldn't work because there were so many guards who I would bump into at some point. I had to fight. But, with no weapon and no strength against 10 trained guards, it seemed impossible. Those guards could wipe out children my age easily, I was no different. Though I did know how to fight thanks to my karate classes.

The first guard struck a blade towards me. I jumped up and landed on my feet. Another guard was about to poke me with his blade, but I dodged. He was about to strike me again, but I caught his blade and pulled it out of his hand. Did I ever say I had no weapon? Correction. Now I had a blade. I used the blade to block every one of their attacks. I had played Blade Fighting with my friends many times and pretty much won every match.

I saw another blade coming towards me, and I pushed it aside and rolled to the other side on the ground. Then, when I stood up, I saw blood dripping off me and onto the floor. I fell down to my knees and fainted. No wait, this had a completely different sensation. I passed away.

I am dead, at the age of nine, in the year 13059, lived 13050–13059. It's the 24th of June, right? I'm guessing, yeah. Now, at least, I don't need to worry about anything, nothing at all. Though, what will Kelly think? Will she burst into tears? I can picture her, sitting on her knees, tears flowing down her face every time she hears my name. And Mum, she will feel worse. She'll probably start sobbing every time she sees a child, and maybe get herself into great danger by trying to go after the voice I had heard.

I couldn't feel myself. My soul suddenly went out of my body, turning into a spirit. My heartbeat stopped. Oxygen wouldn't enter my body through my nostrils. I wasn't living to get chills down my spine. None of my senses worked: touch, hearing, sight, taste, smell, none. My mind wasn't working. My muscles weren't moving. My nostrils weren't smelling death. My tongue couldn't taste the evilness of that place. My eyes couldn't see the mist of darkness and sorrow looming above me. My eardrums wouldn't allow sound particles through it for me to hear the chilling breeze floating through the air. My mind wouldn't allow anything inside it.

Silence. My heart was still.. I didn't know what was going on around me, but one thing was for sure, I was dead, not moving, maybe being stabbed harder to check if I was alive.

The next second, I was in a pitch-black place. It was very murky; I couldn't even see if there was anything in front of me. I kept walking. Nothing came in my way. Maybe there wasn't anything there, at all. I continued walking. The place seemed endless. Suddenly, I realised that as I was walking, I was returning to the same place I was in before.

If this was the place one went after death, I might have never gotten out. I looked at myself; I was a glowing spirit. Did that mean I was a light source? I stretched my arms in front of me to get some light. Things brightened a little, but I still couldn't see things properly. Just a sofa. And a table. The table was laden with delicious fruits and food. There was also a huge jug of water. My stomach grumbled after looking at the food. I moved forward. Sadly, I came back to the same spot I was in. I tried again. No luck. I kept trying.

Suddenly, I heard a voice. "Face eternal darkness, girl. Too bad you can't go into the better afterlife. It's only for respectful people. Martyrs. People who have done good deeds. What have you done? Been disrespectful to your mom. Never cared for your twin, only fought with her — called her a nerd, bookworm. Your dad — you barely talk to him. You were always thinking about yourself. A selfish girl that your mother has given birth to. When you go to your community park, you and your friends always bully friends of Kelly. Now, you get to feel eternal darkness. There is no one here who cares for you," the voice said.

"No! I've done good things too. I saved many people on that underwater ride. I risked my life to get food for those people," I countered.

"You got food at the risk of disobeying your mother, making her worried. All you wanted was to be a hero, to impress people."

Tears started flowing down my cheeks. I felt like a bad girl. I felt guilty. This is what I got. My forever-lasting punishment. Now, all I could do was sit there, for all eternity. I lay down and closed my eyes and soon fell asleep. Unfortunately, I didn't get a single dream. All I got were nightmares.

Kelly was standing, saying something to me. "What a horrible sister you are!"

Then, Mom came in. "I have given birth to such a selfish girl!"

Then, my brothers came in. "The only thing we and Kelly agree about is what a terrible person you are. You never thought about us!"

They kept repeating the same thing over and over again. The voices started overlapping. Soon it was just a bunch of jumbled words that showed how bad I was.

Suddenly, I woke up, panting. Still, I was in eternal darkness. Who knew how many days had passed? Maybe ten. Maybe a whole century. The concept of time was very hard to follow there. I tried walking again.

This time, I could walk, and I was not returning to where I was. But then, my spirit wasn't glowing anymore. Wow. I could walk, but I didn't have light. I looked above me. The ceiling (if there was one) looked more like a sky. It looked like a sky with red stars. It wasn't navy blue, but pure black.

"I need light!" I moaned. "I need light! I need light!"

"Sure, you want light? I can give you light," the same voice said.

Suddenly, the whole place turned lit. The only problem was, the light was blinding. If I opened my eyes, I wasn't able to see in the light, forget about the dark. Even with my eyes tightly shut, they burned.

"On second thought, I think I prefer the dark!" I insisted.

"Are you sure? You seem to be enjoying the light. The pain in your eyes — it isn't the worst of this place. I can give more..."

"I am 100% sure. Now make it dark."

"Whoops, I forgot how to, sorry!" the voice lied. "By the way, I only let you walk so that you can feel the wrath of this amazing place. It is so boring when you're sitting in one place. Anyways, cheerio, I have to visit that other guy, Marcus!" The voice went quiet.

Great. I can't open my eyes, so I don't know what kind of horrors are waiting for me. I kept walking, spreading my arms around, so I didn't bump into anything. Suddenly, something started dragging me. It felt more like the water itself. It dragged me into the water. It was supposed to be a good thing, considering I could breathe underwater.

The only problem was that I couldn't breathe. I literally couldn't breathe underwater. Now, I realised how it was to not be able to breathe underwater. I struggled. I tried to control the water, but my powers didn't work. I tried to speak but couldn't do that either. After a few seconds, I ran out of air. Then it occurred to me, what would happen if I died there?

I kept trying to go above the surface, but the water wouldn't let me. After a few seconds, I couldn't breathe. *Can spirits even breathe? Maybe they can't in spirit water.*

After what felt like a long time, I woke up in a place that seemed worse than the one I was in before. I could see, thankfully. There was a perfect amount of light. However, the place itself was horrible. Everything there was pointy and sharp. The floor was lava, and I was barefoot. The room had jagged rocks all around.. What I could hear was ear-piercing. There was a never-ending sharp noise that almost blasted through my ears. My feet were now burning badly from the lava-hot rocks. I couldn't bear the pain. Every part of my body was hurting.

How on earth can I feel the rocks? Spirits can't touch anything.

Suddenly, I saw a basket full of fruits. I took a mango. It looked delicious. When I took a bite, it was the grossest thing ever. It was a slime with a rock for a seed. I quickly drank water to wash away the gross slime. Bad idea. The water, I realised, was poison. Suddenly, pain washed over me. I died, again.

This time, I was in a place where, yes, I could see again. I saw people getting tortured for eternity, without dying though.

I heard the voice again. "This is the last place you can go to. It is impossible to die here, but even if you do, you will revive again, right here. So, don't worry. Also, you will be given a personalised punishment. You need to go to punishment 210202342. Got it?"

"Uhh… is that just a random number or is that the number of punishments there are?" I asked.

"There are a trillion punishments. You're lucky to get such a low number. The higher the number, the worse the punishment. Anyways, have a nice day!"

I wondered how I could have a nice day over there. I started walking towards the number I had gotten. I saw people being forced to sit in molten hot lava or acid. Some people were being killed every time they were revived. Some people were being used as punching bags. Some were sitting in the fire. I saw people getting struck by lightning every sixty seconds.

Looking at torture, I got scared. What if I got the worst of it all? After loads of walking, I finally reached my number. A sign said: 210202342. I took a deep breath and reluctantly went into my torture area.

"Welcome to torture method 210202342. In this area, you will be fed to a dragon every time you revive. It is as simple as that!" The voice came again.

Fed to a dragon? A dragon! I was panicking as if I were about to be fed to a dragon, which I was.

I saw the dragon up ahead. With every stride, my fear grew. The dragon opened its mouth wide. I could see slime on his teeth. The dragon decided not to swallow me whole, but give me a painful death by munching me up. I am not going to describe this part, because it is disgusting. All I can say is two words. Incredibly painful.

I got revived immediately, which I kind of wished I didn't. This meant the dragon could eat me again.

This time, before the dragon could take a bite, I got electrocuted. As I came out of the electric sensation, I found myself in the place I had been to earlier, the one with poisonous food. I got tempted to eat the food again, but I didn't have time to do so.

I got electrocuted again. Now, I was back in the place with the blinding light.

I got electrocuted one last time.

I heard the same evil, cold voice again. "I told you, I want her alive, not dead. Or else Alice will just choose a new body, and we'll have to start over our capture again. I'll see what to do with you, but first, I'll need to get this foolish girl into the prison cells. Let's see her try to escape that for now. Make sure you do this right or else… And how is the capture of my other teammates going on? I want them captured before Ed can even dare to tell them who they are. It's best they don't know."

I could hear him from a distance. As he spoke, I shivered.

"There are eight rev— I mean, 'of them' we need to capture! It'll take ages before we capture them. Hasn't Master Ed been keeping an eye out so they can't be captured? It's more than impossible — I mean, we're still trying to capture the rest; we're tracking each of them and have already figured out a plan," a man with a feeble voice said.

The cold voice guy seemed to have given the nervous guy a look in the eye.

"Do not say 'Master' Ed! He isn't the Master of me! And, impossible? Impossible, huh? I was able to get a Revenir killed, and you're saying it'll be impossible to get eight more nine-year-olds? I did not get these four scars for nothing! You will make sure I get those eight kids captured in an inescapable room. Now get going!"

"As you wish, Lord Zephyr."

"Wicked people are so hard to find these days!" Lord Zephyr muttered under his breath.

"Lord, what if, in the middle of taking her to the cells, she awakens?"

"That is no problem. She will not wake up until tomorrow."

I heard them speaking from the corner of my ear in the cold room. Suddenly, it occurred to me, *How did I hear it? I am supposed to be in the Land of the Dead!*

No way! Not possible! I could hear my breath floating through the air. The room was filled with evil coldness, sending chills down my spine. Suddenly, two arms grabbed me by my back. I was not someone with patience who could simply keep her eyes closed (so they don't find out I was alive) while some stranger was carrying me to, I don't know where. I opened my eyes and jumped out of the man's arms

I saw in front of me, the man who had grabbed me. A lanky man with fair skin. Freckles covered his face leaving only his forehead and chin. He had jet-black hair that was tied into a small ponytail. His eyes were stone-grey coloured, nose curved, lips cracked, and teeth yellow with black gums. His arms were long and skinny, and his hands looked dirty. He had a bewildered look. Overall, to me, he looked like a bewildered servant, forced into doing the dirty work for Lord Zephyr. The name kept me trembling. I was about to kick him, but he dodged.

"In case you didn't know, I'm Drake, the greatest supporter and servant of Lord Zephyr, trained for years and years. So, make sure you know what you're getting yourself into by fighting me. After many 15-year-olds I have killed, you'd be nothing," the man said, standing up straight, looking more courageous than before.

"Ha! You cowardly man, a great fighter?" I taunt.

"The only person I'm scared of is Zephyr, understand? I'm not scared of you!" he booms.

"Come on, let me finish you off in a sec—" I realised running away would have been better than sarcastically teasing this man.

He kicked my stomach before I realised what he had done. I fell back and felt as if I had broken my ankle during the fall. I got up, and instead of fighting back, I ran.

"Now who's the coward, huh? Come back and fight me, show me you aren't a coward, coward!" he screamed.

I felt a burning sensation rush through my face, but I forced myself to keep running. But then, I tripped over a tripwire and fell. I was in the lair of an evil lord; how did I not expect booby traps? My face smacked the ground and flushed. The bone in my nose felt like it got moulded, and my lips were bleeding. My cheeks turned red due to the pain.

I stood up again. When I turned, I saw Drake running towards me. I started running again, trying to run fast enough so that he couldn't catch up to me. I felt my right arm squeeze. I checked my arm to see that Drake was holding it. I tried wriggling my arm free. Out of all things on his arms, I noticed the date on his watch. No way it was not! I spent seven days here! It was already the 30th of June. Mum would be so worried. The part of my arm that was held by Drake's fist somehow got wet. That made it easier to wriggle free and run.

I kept running. I caught a glimpse of light from far off. My will to go faster increased because it looked like daylight to me. When I reached closer to the light, I saw a hole in the ceiling. I knew I had to climb up, and that it was my only way out. I looked around me. How was I going to get up there? Then, I checked on Drake. He was coming after me.

Next to me, on the brick wall, I saw some bricks popping half an inch out. I thought, if I could climb it, I could get up there. I held a brick and put my leg on another brick. Then, after taking a deep breath, I started climbing. My feet were shaking. There was not enough space to put my feet on, but it was somehow working. When I was about five metres above the ground, the brick under my foot started shaking. I quickly put my leg onto another brick.

I looked towards Drake to see him five metres away from the wall. I started climbing faster. Soon enough, I reached the hole. When I looked down, I saw Drake climbing. He had almost reached me. I stepped onto his hand, and he cried out in pain, losing his balance. He fell down. For some reason, I kind of regretted making him fall.

When I looked around me, I saw that I wasn't anywhere outside but just in another room. I then saw someone in the corner of the room, about my age. She looked weak and sad. Her cinnamon-coloured and short, ragged hair indicated she had stayed here for months.

"Hi," I said.

She turned to me, her lightning-blue eyes gleaming, and smiled. "Hi, I'm Fenna Jockwyn, and you?" she said in a friendly voice.

"I'm your new friend," I said, "Danica Wynter."

"Are you trying to escape this place? I've tried since I was seven, and it never worked out."

"How old are you now?" I asked.

"Nine."

"Well, I've got an idea!"

"Really? What is it?" She looked happier than before.

"Well, you see the hole up there?"

"Yeah…"

"We could climb up to there using the bricked wall, and hopefully, we'd be out of this ridiculous prison."

"Already tried, won't work! The bricks are too small."

"I climbed easily. Maybe this could help." I willed some water from outside the hole to come towards me. In my mind, I pictured it as a sharp ice stick, and it turned into an ice stick. I handed it over to Fenna.

"Perfect!" she exclaimed.

We both started climbing the wall. It was way simpler because we weren't followed by Drake. We were still trying to go quickly in case we were being followed.

Fenna reached up first, and this time, we were in a wooden room with tall walls that were crooked. Being tall, it was also very tapered. It was as if we were inside a hollow tree. It was a roofless room because we could see daylight gleaming from up above.

We started climbing the walls. It was easy because it was basically like tree climbing. This time, I reached first and sat on a thick and durable branch waiting for Fenna. When she was a metre away, her leg slipped. She was about fall, but I instinctively offered my hand for her to clasp. I pulled her up, though it was a little hard. We jumped down and landed on our feet like cats.

Now, where to? We didn't know exactly what place it was. We had ended up in a forest, next to the same dead tree I had seen in a few of my dreams. Fenna and I had started wandering around, trying to figure out where we were.

-5-

The hut

I kept walking, trying to stay next to Fenna. It felt good to have someone as company. I felt the warm, fresh air soothing my skin.

I didn't want to go back to the dead tree. Even being close to it, a spooky atmosphere seemed to slide through my body.

I could sense that there was some life in the forest. Some person was in there. Someone I felt like I knew strongly. I even felt like I knew Fenna as if we were friends since kindergarten, though we weren't. But, there was someone else there, someone I knew well and admired.

There was water on the sand, spilt in a thin trail. But, something seemed weird about the water. It was not mixing with the sand; it was sitting on it.

"Fenna, this isn't normal, is it? The water is not mixing with the sand," I asked, in a confused tone.

"I don't think so. Let's see what it leads to," she replied.

At least, it was good to know that my eyes weren't playing tricks on me.

We followed the trail right to the bait. Guess what the bait was? My Karate teacher! I mean seriously, my karate teacher turned up out of nowhere!

He was a muscular man with skin the colour of pale ivory. He had short hair — the colour of dark chocolate. He had no beard, and his eyes were dark brown.

"Good afternoon, Master Ed," I greeted him.

Fenna also said the same thing. Was he also her tutor?

"Hello, why not come with me once?" He didn't wait for us to answer and just went on. Fenna and I quickly looked at each other and then followed. We passed through a clear path.

After walking for a few minutes, we saw a hut. It was like any ordinary hut, made of tree logs and straws. There was a puddle on the right side of the house. Next to it was a boy the same age as me, apparently drinking water. He looked agile but short. His skin was rose beige, and he had short cedar colored hair. His eyes were stone grey. When I got closer, I realised that right after he took water from the pond and kept the bucket beside him, the pond would automatically refill, and the bucket would get empty. It surprised me.

When I went inside the hut, it looked way more spacious. There were six mattresses and six people. On one of the mattresses, Kelly was sleeping. I was so relieved that she was okay.

On the mattress next to Kelly slept a petite girl with pale ivory skin. She had tortilla-coloured, short, bushy, and unkempt hair that reached her shoulders, and ruby lips.

The first thing I did was wake up Kelly. She woke up instantly, and we tightly hugged each other.

"Danica! What happened? Where have you been? I missed you!" She sounded so worried.

I told her exactly what had happened since the time I woke up and found myself in a small room.

"Where is Mum, by the way?" The second I asked that question, tears dropped from Kelly's eyes.

My karate teacher also looked miserable. The spirit of happiness had strayed away.

"What happened? Where is Mum? What's wrong?" I asked. I was so confused and worried.

"I can't say it. Ask Master Ed, please." She was crying badly. Tears started making a puddle on the mattress.

"Your mother," he sighed, "has perished."

I dropped to my knees. It seemed like everything inside me had vanished, and I had become hollow. I felt like there was nothing worth living for. My mum was dead… dead… dead… Every part of me was wishing this was just a dream. I sat there. I was feeling lonely. Broken. Worthless. Hopeless. My situation could be described in thousand other gruesome words. I just wanted to lie down and pass out. There was nothing left inside me. Nothing but despair. Pictures of my mum flashed through my mind.

My mother can't be dead. She can't. I felt like there was no point in me living anymore. I shouldn't have revived from the dead. I was better off there, not knowing about my mother's situation. My legs trembled. My hands cushioned my face and hid my tears.

My mother, someone who cared for me, someone who loved me, someone who made me feel better, someone who… Now she's dead. I'll never see her again. Never. I sat there for hours and hours.

"Danica, please, it's okay. It'll be alright," Kelly said, still sounding glum but trying not to show it.

"It will be alright? How can anything be alright?"

"I didn't mean tha– "

"Mum died, and you're saying it's okay."

"Danica!" Kelly whined.

"Well, think again! Because it is not alright." A gust of anger snaked down my spine. I could feel the heat on my cheeks.

"You have got to let things go. Don't be caught up in things and forget yourself."

"Let things go? How am I supposed to let go of the fact that Mum died? How can you? I thought she was your mum too. You can't just let things go so easily. It is not how things work!" I said, my throat burning with anger. My face was sticky with the tears that had flooded the hut.

I stomped to another mattress. The second I dropped onto it, I fell asleep. This time, I didn't have any dreams.

When I woke up the next morning, I felt a little peaceful. Master Ed had already cooked us food.

When I asked him how he had gotten the delicious tortilla chips and the tomato salsa, he said, "It's just a little food secret of mine. Now eat up!"

"Hi, what's your name?" I asked the girl who was sleeping next to Kelly last afternoon.

"I'm Alassia Chase," she said.

She had a beautiful pair of sea-green eyes and spoke with a soft, kind voice.

"I'm Danica Wynter."

There was an odd silence.

Then I went to see Kelly, who was sitting on her mattress with her arms folded around her knees.

"Hi," Kelly said silently.

Sitting beside her, I sighed. "I was wondering, how did it happen?"

"According to Master Ed, hunger. I wasn't there to give her food. She couldn't get out of the bubble."

"Oh yeah," I said, my face still looking down.

"Wait a second, what do you mean you weren't in the bubble while I was away?" I asked. Had she gone through horrible stuff, too?

"No, I woke up in a cage. I couldn't see anything outside because I was handcuffed to the floor, facing the opposite side. I couldn't find a way to get the handcuffs off me. I tried pulling it with the opposite hand. I tried using my hands to budge the chain that was connected to the floor. I tried a couple of other things.

A few hours passed, and then I realised I could draw on the metal with my nails. I tried. I ended up with a knife. I used it to cut off the handcuffs. Next, I drew a hairpin and tried to undo the lock on the cage. I struggled a little, but then I finally got it. The cage slid open, and I stepped out.

The coast was clear. Crystal clear. I ran one way and saw a man coming. So, I ran the other way, and that man started chasing me. Finally, I reached an exit and found myself in a forest. Then, I bumped into Azteque and Alassia, and we found our way here."

"Azteque?" I asked.

She pointed at the same boy who was drinking water from the pond earlier.

Three new people entered with Master Ed. I guessed that they went through a similar adventure.

One of them was a lithe girl with sienna skin. She had jet-black hair with curls that were quite disarrayed. She had cobalt grey eyes, and her lips were cracked and dry. She introduced herself as Lezabel Grande.

Next to her, there was a lanky boy with beige skin. He had cocoa-coloured, pompadour hair that was tidy. His eyes were dark brown. He said his name was Franz Scheller.

Next to him was a little boy who claimed to be Davian Wolf. He had dark chocolate hair that was styled like spikes. He had honey-coloured skin and his eyes glinted sea green.

That night, we all had fun; we sat around a campfire, roasting marshmallows and chatting.

-6-

Old Man's Tale

Ugh! Why can't I beat Fenna? I kept whining in my mind.

Fenna and I had been racing, and I hadn't beaten her once.

Behind me, someone said, "Well, don't be upset about being slow! You have other great qualities." It was Master Ed.

"How did you know what I was thinking?" I asked, quite shocked. I hadn't said that out loud, definitely!

His eyes widened. "Well… I think you guys ought to know the truth. Huddle up, everybody!"

Kelly, Azteque, Alassia, Lezabel, Franz, and Davian quickly joined us.

"I am sure you all are aware of the *Legend of the World Bomb*. I am also sure you all know who Edward Rev and Rowana King are. Well, you should know that Edward is the full form of Ed."

"Hahaha! There are many Eds in this world! How come you're specifically Edward Rev? Plus, Edward Rev died millennia ago," I said. There was no way I was going to believe that.

"I'm immortal," he told us.

"Yeah, and I am superwoman!" I countered.

"You actually do have powers, by the way. But first, do you want me to prove myself?" he asked.

I nodded, and he pulled out a sword. I was about to stop him but then decided to let him go through with it. Without hesitation, he stuck the sword right through his heart. I saw the blade of the sword turning to dust. Slowly, his whole body was turning to dust, until there wasn't a single part of Master Ed left. My eyes widened. Horror-struck, I screamed. I put my hand through the dust.

The dust flew from my hand and back onto the ground. The dust started forming the shape of a man standing. Eventually, there was an actual man standing there.

"Master Ed! But… But how? You're dead!" I exclaimed.

"So, as I was saying, I lived even before the World Bomb. A time when mythical creatures were still at Earth's core. A time when there were no Enchanted Isles. I was just a happy boy living a happy life. It all changed when my dad exiled me from London. I had to leave the city with no one willing to come with me.

"One night, I was just sleeping in the dark forest, when I saw a glint of light, glimmering, from the corner of my eye. I went to check it. In front of me, I saw a harp. It was a harp made of gold. I thought of playing it for a while as music calms me down sometimes. So, I flicked the thin rope. Just as I did so, the harp started playing on its own, creating a magical tune. I could see magical dust around as if I was in a fairy tale. The dust disappeared after a while.

"I didn't understand what just happened, but I decided not to think about it. However, as days passed, I started experiencing strange things. Whenever, I went swimming in the lake or took a bath, I realised I could breathe underwater. Slowly, different powers started showing up, and so, I planned to teach myself how to control it.

"I stayed in the forest by myself for a few years, and then the World Bomb happened. I somehow saved myself and met Rowana on the journey. Then, as you know, we had nine children. Each of these children was capable of doing different things. One of them was Felix whose eyesight was so good, he could see the sun up close." He looked at Franz.

"Romeo could disappear and reappear, and he could do the same to other people and things." He looked at Azteque.

"The water responded to Alice." He looked at me.

"Merrick could travel to the past or future." He looked at Davian.

"Eileen could turn into different animals." He looked at Alassia.

"Ginny could strike lightning out of her fingers." He looked at Fenna.

"If Tenessa drew something, it would come out alive." He looked at Kelly.

"Hecate would know what someone was thinking." He looked at Lezabel.

"If Morsius died, he would come back to life." This time, he didn't look at anyone, just sighed.

"All these children had powers that were derived from their dad. Which means…

"I have all these powers, plus one more. The guardian power. I am the guardian of these nine children. I have the power of taking away anyone's power." He paused, letting us take in all of this. Then, he continued, "Why am I telling you all this? Because all these nine kids grew up and died. Then, their spirits released and took the form of another body. This cycle has continued for ten millennia until you guys. I'm guessing, by now, you all would have figured out your powers?"

"Super sight!" Franz says.

"Teleporting!" Azteque says.

"Water!" I exclaim!

"Time twisting!" Davian says.

"Shape shifting!" Alassia says.

"Lightning!" Fenna says.

"Art shifting!" Kelly says.

"Telepathy!" Lezabel says.

"Correct! Have you ever gotten a weird feeling, and then, after that, you're not controlling your body? It's because the spirit inside you is controlling you."

"How did Morsius die? Isn't he immortal?" I asked.

"I took away his powers," Master Ed said.

"Why? I mean you wouldn't just go like, 'Hey, you're starting to bore me. I'll take away your powers!'" I asked.

"Well, most of the immortals savage their power and think that they're unstoppable. Morsius thought so too and killed Alice and Ginny," he said.

I widened my eyes. Why would someone want to kill their own sister? I stared at Kelly with dread, making a silent vow to never kill her.

"And, what about the immortal who lives now?" I asked.

"His name is Zephyr Foros."

Zephyr… The name gave me the creeps.

"When I was captured by him, he said something about *Revenirs*, what is that?" I asked.

"My full name is Edward Revenir. My kids called themselves the Revenirs."

"Why exactly are we here though?" I asked.

"Zephyr is a really greedy immortal and will do anything in his power to take my place and become the guardian. When he does, not only the Revenirs, but the whole world will be doomed, and we cannot let that happen. I need you guys to train and master your powers so you can stop him," Master Ed explained.

My head was overflowing with the questions I had, but then Master Ed said, "Enough information for today. You all should go and take some rest now."

"Can I call you Guardian Ed?" I asked.

"No, Master Ed is fine." He rolled his eyes.

"Ed-dian?"

"Nope."

"Aww darn!"

I kept thinking about everything that had happened till now. Considering all the curiosities I had, I realised I had been through a lot.

One second, I was playing in the water park; the next second, I was making barriers out of the water. How is that even possible? How come nobody knows of us Revenirs? How come my karate teacher turns out to be such a powerful superhuman? How on earth did I never realise that I can breathe underwater? How can a harp make you so powerful? I just trailed off into my thoughts, until I dozed off into a deep sleep.

-7-

Training

I was woken up the next day by Master Ed. He called us all outside the hut.

"What happened?" Kelly asked.

"Why are we here?" Alassia questioned.

"I want to sleeeeep!" Davian whined.

"It's five in the morning!" I said.

"Even the sun isn't up!" Franz exclaimed.

"Once all of you are quiet, we can start," Master Ed said.

Everyone sealed their lips and waited for him to explain.

"We're going for a morning run," he said.

"That sounds like fun," I exclaimed, sarcastically. "Good night." I turned around and started walking.

"And, all of you are coming," he ordered.

I turned back and joined the group.

Master Ed led the way. One by one, everyone followed. We went through the forests, which looked pretty gloomy since it was still dark.

I heard someone mutter, "When I said I'd stay instead of going home, I did not sign up for this!"

I totally agreed.

My eyelids were closing every half second; I tried to keep up with Master Ed. It was so cold that although I was sweating, I was still freezing. I wanted to stop for some rest after fifteen minutes, but everyone else was long gone, so I had to sprint to catch up.

I turned around to look at Kelly, but I couldn't see her around. I figured her extremely slow legs couldn't keep up with us.

After half an hour, we reached back to the hut. I had never been glad to see a hut as much as I was now.

I was about to go straight to bed, but Master Ed called us back.

"Everyone, sit down around here," he said.

We all sat around him.

"Remember, yesterday I mentioned that Zephyr is a greedy immortal and that you may have to suffer war at some time. Well, Zephyr has been training for over a century for a war. I don't mean to pressure you, but he is really great with his powers and is an amazing fighter. If you guys are in this form in the war, he could kill you guys like ants. So, if you want to win, you're going to have to train. Extremely hard. Every day, you will have to go for morning runs followed by a healthy breakfast — emphasis on healthy — a bit of rest, and then we start practising our powers. Does that sound good?"

"What? You're saying that we'll wake up at five every single day? No way!" I exclaimed.

"Or you guys could die in the war. It is entirely up to you."

"Waking up at five sounds good!" I agreed, reluctantly.

"Well, I bet you all must be starving, I will draw you all some food."

When Master Ed had stated that we would be eating a healthy breakfast from then on, I panicked that I wouldn't get to eat tasty food for who knows how long. Surprisingly, the açai bowl was delicious, and I love fresh fruit juice, so breakfast was nice.

After we were all done eating, we relaxed for a while. I went back to bed to catch around thirty more minutes of sleep.

When it was time to start training, Kelly came into my room, gave me a nudge, and called me outside. I woke up and quickly freshened up. Feeling a lot less tired, I went outside to find everyone waiting for me.

"Now that everyone is here, we can start," Master Ed said. "First, I want to start off by seeing what you can already do. We'll start with…" He looked around. Staring right into Azteque's eyes, he said, "Azteque, come to the front."

He stepped forward.

"I want you to teleport this leaf into this circle," Master Ed said, whilst drawing a circle on the sand right in front of the leaf. "Can you do that?"

Azteque said, "I'll try."

"Okay, bring out your arm and focus on the leaf. Right now, I want you to close your eyes, and imagine the circle with the leaf in it. Move your hand to trace the circle now, and channel as much energy and power as you can," he said.

Azteque was so focused, he was literally shaking. After about two seconds, I saw a green thing in the circle. Only that it was half of the leaf.

"You have understood the concept, the method, and the way of doing it; you just need to be clearer with your imagination. But, that was good," Master Ed said. "Just continue practising that. Now, I want Alassia to come up."

After we moved a little further, so Azteque could practise with more space, Master Ed started Alassia's training.

"Okay, Alassia, let's start small. I want you to turn this needle into a toothpick. Just imagine the needle is a toothpick and put in some effort so you will have your end result."

She put forward her hand, closed her eyes, and when she opened them, she looked for the needle on the floor. Instead, she found a feather.

We moved on further to allow Alassia to practise, whilst Davian took his turn. He was asked to make us go back one minute in time to when Alassia did the transformation. Instead, he managed to make us go only a few seconds in the past when Master Ed was briefing Davian about this task.

Next was Franz's turn. He had to check what number was written on the paper Master Ed stuck on his back. He was extremely focused but saw only the 1 in 21.

Fenna had to use her lightning powers to burn a leaf, which she missed by a few inches. Kelly had to draw a a flower and make it come alive, but the stem didn't materialise. Lezabel had to figure out what Master Ed was thinking, and according to him, she was close but not correct. Finally, it was my turn.

"Now, I want you to put your hand in front of you, spread your fingers, and focus on the water in the lake; try to channel it. Feel its energy, feel the waves, and the movements. Feel it flow through your veins. Now, imagine a ball made of water. Imagine the ball rising from the lake. Yes, that's it. While imagining that, move your hand slightly upwards, to gesture the rise. Hmm good, you're getting there," Master Ed said.

My hands were literally shaking because of the amount of force I was using. I could feel the cold, soothing water as if it was flowing in me. I imagined a ball of water slowly rising from the lake, and I slowly moved my hand upwards, still focusing all my energy on the water. The ball was slowly coming up, and by the time half of it emerged from the water, it burst.

"Okay, well, we need to work on control and channelling your thoughts, but otherwise it was a really good first try. Keep practising," Master Ed commented.

"Thanks."

After that, Master Ed drew us some lunch. Once we were done, it was time for hunting. Master Ed took us into the forest.

We hid behind a bunch of bushes, watching a doe. Master Ed made me go first. He gave me a sword and pushed me in front of the doe.

"Remember, think like your opponent."

Obviously, she would run away. I tried running after her, getting close enough to stab it with the sword. I lifted the sword and stabbed the doe. She fell to the ground in pain. But, only then did I realise that I only managed to cut off its tail. Before the doe could get up and make a run for it, I stabbed her again, and she stopped moving.

After everyone else was done with the hunting, we went back to the hut and started our fitness session. We started off with a warm-up, and then did a bit of running. Next, we played football, and finally, climbed trees. This part of the day was the only thing I was good at because it didn't involve my powers or disturb my sleep.

Our daily routine was the same for about half a year until we finally mastered the basics. I was at last able to make a ball of water, create shapes out of it, and control where it went. I once splashed Fenna by levitating a water ball over her head and releasing it. Of course, the payback was worse because she then used her electro-magic on me. Moral of the day: Never ever mess with a girl with lightning powers.

I was getting used to waking up at five, and now, even Kelly was able to catch up during our morning runs.

By the end of the first year, I perfected my aim; I could run a mile without stopping, and I could kill animals without making a sound.

By the end of two years, I could kill two or three animals at a time, transform water into any shape, and easily direct water to move in any direction.

Present...

After another day of intensive practice, I go to sleep. For ages, I haven't had a dream about my lookalike, but today, I do.

She holds out a book. It is dusty and sea blue. The cover has some designer border etched, and it says — The Future of Water. It looks just about 100 pages long. Suddenly, it glows. It glows a lighter version of sea blue on the etched parts.

Suddenly, I wake up with a start.

"What was my lookalike trying to show me?" I mutter to myself.

"What dream did you have this time?" Master Ed asks me, sitting on a wooden chair he carved.

"I saw my lookalike. You'd know with your mind-reading power stuff," I say, looking up at him.

"I do, but it's not always good to read people's minds without their consent. By the way, that girl was Alice."

I nod. "So, do you know what Alice was trying to show me?"

"Yes, Merrick once gifted Alice a book because she'd saved him from drowning in the sea. The book is very powerful, and it can never be ripped. Whenever it glows, it means that the book has been updated and new content has been added."

"But, what does the title mean? *The Future of Water*," I ask.

"I'm getting to that. Do you remember what power Merrick had?"

"Yes, I think, he is a Time Twister, right?"

He nods. "Yes, he is. So, he used his powers to make a book of prophecies about all the people who had Alice's spirit. That's why the title *The Future of Water.*"

'Oh yeah! The future (as in the prophecy) and water (all the people with Alice's spirit). But then, it glowed. That means new content has been added. The only content that could have been added is a prophecy about me. I must get my hands on that book before anyone else does.'

"I need to make sure everyone is safe, that includes you. Meanwhile, you need to ensure that no one gets their hands on the book. I think I'll ask the others to join us in looking for it," he says.

"Okay," I say. I don't even want to go searching alone. Where exactly do you —"

"I am not sure. It could be anywhere on Earth. I can't really locate it," he says, putting his hand on the ground.

"So, are we going or not?" I ask.

"Complete your practice and get some sleep. We leave for the book-hunt in a few days," he says. "I'll inform the rest."

I simply nod and move on.

We all practice for some time, training as hard as we can. Soon enough, it is nightfall. We all go to sleep. The next day, an adventure awaits.

-8-

The Future of Water

When I wake up the next morning, everyone else is still asleep. I decide to do some practice. I start off with some basics like conjuring a floating ball out of water. I hold my hand out, my fingers spread wide, in front of the lake. I focus all my energy on the water. I gradually move my hand upwards, the ball of water following my movement. I let go of my force, and the water goes splashing back into the lake.

Next, I try to practise freezing water. I lay my hand a foot or two above the water. I exhale air out of my mouth, and slowly, start raising my hands, making the water rise. I gesture for the water to flow toward me. I exert my strongest willpower to turn it to ice. No luck. I gesture for the water to go back into the lake. I try again. But this time, I only pull a small amount of the water. It keeps floating in the air. I touch the floating blob of water.

"Please work!" I mutter to myself.

I will the water turn into ice. Again, nothing happens.

Agitated, I scream at the water, "Turn to ice already!"

As expected, nothing.

"Turn to ice," I scream louder, stomping my foot.

Unexpectedly, the water turns to ice! Not that I'm complaining, but how did that happen now? I didn't do anything but let anger leak. Strong emotions! In this case: Anger.

I try again. I make my emotions get stronger. Suddenly, I feel something cold in my hands. I open my eyes to check it. There is a ball of ice sitting on my palm. But, there is something weird about it. It's a thin layer of ice, but the core is water. It resembles the toy-balls that have water in them, the ones I used to get from Toy Store-y (the shop down the lane from where I used to live).

"Seriously? So much for getting a ball of ice?" I scream angrily at the ice.

With bitterness, I smash the ice to the ground and stomp on it. Then, I take a deep breathe. Inhale. Exhale. *Okay. I'll try again.*

I repeat the process of turning the water into ice. Though, this time, I use force. I keep trying. Trying.. I continue until all the energy is drained out of me, and I fall onto the ground.

I groan, "I quit!"

I walk back to the tents and get some sleep. As I fall onto the bed, my muscles loosen up. In less than a millisecond, I was asleep. Luckily, I had a dreamless sleep.

When I wake up, the next day, my body feels better. I have had just enough rest. My day goes by practising.

Try 1: Nothing.

Try 2: No better.

Try 3: Little bit of water turns into ice, but the rest is still water.

Try 4: No ice!

Try 5: The crust is ice, but the core is water.

Try 6: Can I never have full ice? The core is ice, but the crust is water.

Try 7: Back to zero!

Try 8: Nothing. I give up!

Pretty much no progress. Eight tries, and I end up with a small puddle of water on the ground and two balls — one's core is ice and the other's crust is ice. My energy level goes down.

"One last time!" I mutter to myself.

My emotions reach the peak point. This time, I manage to create a ball of ice.

Then I try to do a few more challenging exercises. I, once again, hold my hand out, in front of the water, and focus all my energy on the water. I gesture for a few balls of water to rise. This time, I don't let go. Instead, I start pulling my fingers towards each other, to gesture the balls to get slimmer, like the shape of an arrow. I spread my fingers again and make the water freeze into ice. I look towards my aim — a few trees, and swing my arm with powerful force, towards the target. The arrows, following my gestures, and move towards the trees. Three of them hit the bullseye, one misses barely, and the last hits the wrong tree. I try the same exercise a few more times until all five arrows hit the correct trees.

After practice, I decide to make a weapon that can help me on the journey. The first weapon that comes to my mind is a boomerang, something I have always wanted to have. It's fascinating — there's just something about the way it works, and how it always returns to the owner. Besides, I have always wanted to recreate one of those scenes in movies where someone throws a boomerang at the enemy, and they dodge, but twenty seconds later, it returns out of nowhere and knocks the enemy from behind.

I put my hand out in front of the lake, spread my fingers, and gesture for a ball of water to rise. I turn the ball into the shape of a boomerang. Once I perfect the shape, I freeze it.

Soon enough, everyone else is also awake. Everyone quickly freshens up, and we set to leave.

We decide to find any source of water we can in the forest.

"Definitely not in this pond," I say, without even checking it. For some reason, I can just feel the book is not there.

The water in the pond we are looking into starts splashing towards our right. I don't really know how it happened because I haven't told the water to do that.

"What was that about?" Kelly says.

Everyone looks at me as if I were the culprit of a crime.

"I didn't do it!" I say. "Wait a second, why don't we follow the water? It splashed that way, which means..."

We start walking towards our right, to a lake at some distance. When we reach closer, the lake-water doesn't splash at all. It simply stays still. Silence. I study the water, carefully, and see a glint of light right at the bottom. However, I know it's not the book.

"I'm going in," I say.

Everyone tries to protest, but it's too late. I'm already underwater. Still breathing, still dry, but I'm underwater.

I keep going deeper. Deeper. Deeper. When I reach the bottom, I realise that I was correct. The glint of light is not the book. I see a glowing underwater herb. It looks like rainbow thyme. I swim towards it to examine the thyme; it looks ordinary, just that it's has a shine to it. I pluck a leaf, take a deep breath, and drop it in my mouth. Gradually, the view around me turns hazy, and then there is nothing but blackness. Then, I fall unconscious.

Suddenly, I open my eyes. I'm outside the water. Everyone else is glaring at me as if to check if I'm alive.

"H...how long have I been asleep?" I ask.

"For about fifteen minutes to half an hour," Master Ed says.

"Fifteen minutes?" I jump.

"Yes. What happened? Did you find the book?" Kelly asks.

"Well, nope. I did not. Though, I did find a rainbow thyme," I say.

Master Ed widens his eyes.

"Rainbow thyme? As in the tropos thyme?" Master Ed exclaims. "Did you eat it?"

"Yes, I did! Was I not supposed to?"

"Awesome! Now, where do we need to go, Danica?" he asks me.

Why me?

"That way, towards left." I don't know how I figured that out, but I somehow just did.

We end up somewhere outside the forest, in a desert. Every step on the steaming, grainy sand makes me feel like I am getting sucked into it. There are no flowers, no roads, no animals, no butterflies, and no water. Just total nothingness. My throat is already dry under the boiling hot sun.

"The Bila Nihaya desert! Located in Epizeur in Auberfort! I've always wanted to visit Auberfort!" Kelly says.

"How on earth are we supposed to find water in this desert?" I ask.

Water in a desert does not make any sense. The book can only be in the water, so…?

We keep walking and walking. The sizzling sun roasts us on our way. Water droplets drip from my forehead. I haven't drunk water for so long. For me, no water means no fuel because water is what runs me. My feet feel like lead and so does the rest of my body. Still, I force myself to continue and keep walking.

Suddenly, my legs interfere with my brain. They take control of me. They make me, unwillingly, go towards a cactus. I think it's because of the book, but I realise that there is no water here — just granular sand and green cactus. The cactus was as normal as ever. Thorns coming out of its beefy body. Inside its body, there would be water stored, as usual. Wait a second… water? That's it!

"Guys, I think I know where the book could be," I say, full of excitement. But, there is no answer. "Guys?"

I turn around to see no one.

"How could they just leave me?" I mutter to myself.

I start tracing my footsteps. They are very faint because of the wind, but will still do as long as I can see them. I keep running. I slash through the wind. Suddenly, I can't control myself. My legs move by themselves, and are not under my mind's command anymore. I somehow start going the wrong way, not the way the footsteps lead to. I keep going straight. My body seeks water.

Soon enough, I smell water. My hands tremble with excitement. What if the book is here?

I dive into the freshwater. A calm feeling settles over me. My throat is still feeling dry and screaming for water. I open my mouth slightly to allow the water to enter. The water tasted much better than anything I had tasted in the past, at least much better than my sweat. Only when I start choking on the water, I realise I had kept my mouth open for too long. I swim to the surface and cough the water out. When I feel better, I dip my face back underwater. Pure silence. I see through the clear water. There is a whole new world full of creatures. Some glossy pearls, fallen out of the oysters, catch my eyes. I gaze at the shiny plants all around. The fish, swimming around calmly, do not seem to notice me. However, I must stop gazing around and start searching. I check behind the plants. Every time I disturb a bush, fish come out. Two minutes pass. No luck. Five minutes pass. No luck. Ten minutes pass. No luck. Fifteen minutes pass. No luck. Half an hour pass…

I am now deep into the oasis, still not out of the water. I keep checking around.

"Whoops! Sorry, Sir. I was just searching for lost property," I say as I bump into a man.

Why am I going about telling others that I'm searching for something underwater? And, who exactly would be underwater right now? I look up.

"Wait a second, oh, I didn't notice you're here, Master Ed! Where is everyone else? And, how come you somehow happen to be here?" I ask. I am so relieved to have company.

"Well, we split up. The kids went to find you again, and I came to find the book," he says.

If they split up, doesn't that mean…

"Another year of finding them? Oh, come on!" I say.

He gestures to me a 'no'. "I know exactly where they are. We just need to teleport from here to them. They are back in the Bila Nihaya desert, by the way."

I touch his arm, and he takes me to the Bila Nihaya desert. It is hot, and extremely dry.

I see my friends leaning down, huffing from the exhaustion of walking in the hot weather. Suddenly, Kelly spots me. I don't know what she said, but they all speed up towards me as if they had never been tired.

"Danica," they all cry.

"You know, we've been looking for you all day," Franz complains.

"Yeah! What held you back?" Kelly asks me.

"My legs started controlling me and took me towards a cactus. I figured that the cactus has water, which means that the book could be there. However, when I turned around to tell you, you weren't there! Then, I went searching for you and ended up in freshwater. I decided to search for the book in the water. But, instead of finding the book, I found Master Ed."

"Let's continue our search. We've got no time to waste," Master Ed says, "Is the book in the desert, Danica?"

"No, we need to go into the city," I say, still not sure how I know that. The words just dropped out of my mouth.

Master Ed nods.

"Oh my god! Do we need to walk all the way there? That'll take us years," Lezabel whines.

"Not with me! Touch me. Actually, let's give Azteque a chance. He has the teleporting power," Master Ed says.

"No! I am not so good at it. I might just end up getting us into a dustbin and making a fool of myself," Azteque says, looking mousy.

We all give him an encouraging look.

"Ugh! Fine, I'll do it."

We all touch him. He takes a deep breath. We all are now teleporting with him. Suddenly, I figure that I'm falling. Falling? I look down to find out that we are dropping into the city, from the sky. My hair stands tall as gushes of wind slash through my body. My brain feels dizzy. My hands shiver. I hear my heart beating louder than a drum. I try grabbing Kelly's hand but she's too far. Everyone is falling. Fast. Faster. The wind covers my ears tightly, but I hear Master Ed booming.

"Hold each other's hands!" he yells.

We form a circle. I look down. We are so close to land. The fear inside me swells. My insides clamour. I am one metre above a car. Half a metre. Twenty-five centimetres. Ten centimetres. Five centimetres. Two centimetres. I'm on the top of the car. Though I haven't crashed. I am standing on the roof of the car. We all are. Master Ed must have taken over the teleporting.

The car isn't moving now. I pray the traffic signals don't turn green. I get ready to jump off the car. Suddenly, I lose balance. The car starts moving. I see the traffic signals. It's green. Now what? I'm not an expert who can jump off a moving car. Suddenly, a hoverboard comes darting towards me. I catch it mid-air. I hold onto it and pull myself upwards. It moves on its own, somehow. While the others struggle to maintain balance, the hoverboard safely lands me on the pavement. It then goes back to picking everyone else one by one. After everyone is on the pavement, I realise someone is missing.

"Where's Alassia? Alassia!" I bellow.

Suddenly, the hoverboard turns into a girl. She looks like… Alassia. Shapeshifter.

"You just saved our lives," I say to Alassia.

I look at Azteque. He looks downwards with a sad face.

"If it weren't for you, we'd have to walk to the city with lead-like legs," I say to Azteque, trying to encourage him, and pat him on the back.

"You did great!" Master Ed adds.

"Thanks," he says. His mood is still downcast, but he smiles.

Master Ed looks at me. I understand what he wants to say.

"We need to keep going straight," I say, "but first, can we stop for food?" My stomach has been growling for quite some time now.

"Yeah. I'm hungry."

"Me too!"

"Same!"

"Okay. There is a restaurant here called Lucy Lunch. It has pizza, pasta, spaghetti…" Franz says.

Everyone stares at him blankly. They seem to ask him how he knows.

"What? I've got super sight, remember?"

"Oh yeah! Now, are we going? Or do you want me to eat you up?" I ask.

Franz chuckles and takes us to the restaurant.

It looks small with just a few seats, a cashier, and a fridge with ice cream. The thing that tempted me the most was the waterberry ice cream. Waterberry is like mulberry, but it's grown underwater. We order pasta and spaghetti, and I order a waterberry ice cream.

As I take a bite, my stomach gets a feels-way-better feeling. One hour later, I am done enjoyably licking up the ice cream and devouring the meal. We leave the restaurant and reluctantly continue our search.

Looking at everyone else's faces, I can tell that they all didn't really want to come with me to find the prophecy book. I felt angry at myself. How could I have made everyone do dangerous and tiresome things for something that is my responsibility?

We continue going straight. A question suddenly pops in my mind.

"How am I able to tell which way the book is? I've known it all along," I ask Master Ed.

"The magic of the tropos thyme. The rainbow thyme you ate back in the forest," he says.

It makes sense. The tropos thyme provides a path to finding what you're truly looking for.

We keep walking on the pavement. Suddenly, I smell a faint scent of magical water. The scent is getting a little stronger with every step I take. We pass a few shops, bakery stores, and restaurants. Auberfort is quite ancient. There are no flying cars around, only land cars. The street lamps don't work on electricity; they are fire lamps that people light up whenever the sun falls. I have heard tales about Auberfort. It used to be a desert, long ago. Some parts of the desert still exist, like the Bila Nihaya.

As I walk, admiring the villages and ancient monuments, I realise that the faint scent of magic water is not faint anymore. The scent has grown stronger.

After ten more minutes of speed walking, I can't take it anymore. The scent is disturbing my eyes, and poisoning my face. My hands press the sides of my head. My insides squeal. A cold, icy sensation gusts down my spine. I feel like yelling, but the scent blocks my throat.

"What's wrong, Danica? What happened?" I hear Kelly saying.

"I'm guessing it's the scent of the book stinging her,which means the book is somewhere... in that lake!" Master Ed exclaims. "You all go somewhere far with Danica, I'll fetch the book."

My eyes are still closed, struggling. We walk far away from the book now. My body is slowly starting to heal. My throat isn't stinging anymore. Cold chills aren't running down my spine. I gradually open my eyes.

We are sitting in a café. We wait for about fifteen minutes. Suddenly, Master Ed appears out of nowhere. I cross my fingers in the hope that he has the book. My eyes fall on his hands. He is holding a sea-blue book with water designs on it. He hands it to me. I take the book, not taking my admiring eyes off it. The book looks small in width and length, but by the number of pages, I can tell that this book has a prophecy about everyone who has ever controlled water. The book suddenly starts shining, emitting a sea-blue hued light. It is probably because it is with its current master.

I slowly open the book. I flick through the pages until it shows my name, on the top of the second last page.

Danica Wynter
You will be betrayed by a teammate
The one you love will be someone you truly hate
A big battle will come by
Where many will die
Guardian is Morning Star's fate.

"Who is the one to betray us?" Davian asks.

"I don't know, but I'm guessing whoever will betray me is someone I love," I say.

Everyone looks at Kelly.

"No, it's definitely not Kelly! Yes, I love her, and she is one of my teammates, but it can't be Kelly!"

Everyone still eyes Kelly feeling suspicious.

"Hey, please stop staring at me. I would never cause any harm to Danica." Kelly sounds defensive.

"How evil do those blue eyes look to you? Now can we get back to the prophecy? Thank you," I say.

I try to keep my anger only to my throat because any higher would mean that I would spill it right at them.

"'A big battle… Many will die…' That only means one thing — Zephyr. Maybe Zephyr is also the one I get betrayed by. Though he isn't the one I love," I guess.

"I suppose we've got to practice extra if we want to be able to win the war," Kelly suggests.

"Agreed." Alassia nods.

"Now that we've gotten the book, let's go back to the hut," I say.

"No need for that. We've to keep moving so that —" Master Ed looks up. A waiter in a French-type uniform is waiting for us to decide our order, "— so that it's hard for *him* to find us."

"May I take your order for dessert, Sir?" The waiter asks.

"No, thank you. We're —" Master Ed says.

"Two cupcakes, a doughnut, and an ice cream, please!" Davian interrupts.

We all roll our eyes at him.

"Come on, please! Can't we just sit here and eat for a second?"

"I don't have a fortune of money. We're going." Master Ed demands in a way that even Davian didn't continue pleading.

We leave the restaurant and simply follow Master Ed.

"Where are we going to go now? And, by the way, how are we going to get money?" I ask.

Davian grins as if he's gotten a crazy idea.

"I know. Why don't we just borrow money from people?" he says.

"It's known as stealing. You know what else it's called? Illegal," Kelly says.

"I got another idea! Kelly can draw money," Davian exclaims.

"It's known as cheating," Kelly says.

"You got a better idea? If not, you can always come back to me for another crazy idea," Davian says.

"I am never coming to you if you want to cheat, alright?"

"Why not? Instead of getting money from Kelly's art, we could get anything else we want," Master Ed suggests.

Everyone nods in agreement.

-9-

The Imposter

After leaving the café, we arrive at a campsite in Auberfort.

While roaming around, exploring the place, a girl comes up to me and says, “Hi, what’s your name?”

“Hi, I’m Danica, and you are?” I ask.

“Cleo. Nice place isn’t it?”

“Yeah, probably the best holiday I’ve had in a while,” I say. “Oh, and I love the tents and the campfire!”

“Are you going to the picnic tomorrow?” she asks.

“Picnic? What picnic?”

“Yeah, they host a picnic every week.”

“Oh, I’d love to check it out!”

“Do you live nearby?” she asks.

“Uh, no. I live in Glazenia.”

“Oh, I live in the village nearby, so I come to this campsite quite a lot with my parents.”

“Cool! I’ve always wanted to visit the villages of Auberfort. I’ve heard they’re the best villages on the planet. What is it like in the village?”

“Everyone lives united, and there is pretty much everything you need. A cinema, a school, a park, a mall, a few restaurants, and a café.”

"It seems like one of the most perfect places to live."

"Well, what is it like in Glazenia?"

"Well, it's pretty nice over there. There are amazing parks."

We continue talking for a while. It feels so good to make a friend here.

Soon, she leaves as her parents don't like her out late. So I decided to join the rest around the fire. The orange flames dancing on the wood help liven the mood. The ashes float in the air and the bonfire dances while we sit around, lost in our own thoughts.

After a while, I go inside my tent and fall asleep.

Next morning, I feel someone shaking me vigorously. "Kellyyyy, leave me alone!" I groan.

"We better get going for the picnic with normal, non-superhero humans!" Kelly says, full of excitement.

With that, I get off the bed and freshen up instantly. "Now, what are you waiting for? Let's go!"

Fenna, Kelly, and I grin at each other.

We go to the picnic by the hearth of the campsite. Sandwiches. Burgers. French fries. Chips. Juice. Music. You name it, and it was there. How amazing is that! I chit-chat with Fenna. Laughing. Things I haven't done in many, many days.

"What is the date?" I ask Fenna.

"It's 1st July," Fenna says.

"1st July? My birthday is the day after tomorrow! I hope it goes just like today! Except for the dream part; I don't want a scary dream," I say. "Last year's birthday was quite fun! We had cakes, pizza, and burgers. I enjoyed it thoroughly. We laughed. We played games. We danced. We listened to music. I hope this year would be fun too."

"Yeah! Right," Fenna says.

We continue talking for a while. When the sun sets, we start making our way to the tent. Yawning, I go to sleep.

The next day is just the same. Picnic. Fun. I can't stop thinking about tomorrow. Hopefully, it will be a fun birthday. Soon, it is night. I eagerly go to sleep, wanting tomorrow to come quickly.

When I wake up, I am surprised. No one wishes Kelly or me a happy birthday. It is as if they forgot. The whole morning feels normal. In the afternoon, I go to the picnic.

When I reach there, my eyes glow! There is a big outdoor stage and a few circular tables. It's a party décor all around. A woman in a pink dress and a beautiful hairstyle stands in the centre of the stage, holding a mic. Kelly, Fenna, and I go and take a seat. The woman gets her mic closer to her mouth.

"Good afternoon, everybody! Let's welcome the birthday girls, Kelly and Danica! Woohoo!" she says in a very excited voice. "Kelly and Danica, would you like to come on stage?"

We go up to the stage, excited.

"Happy Birthday, Kelly and Danica! Which one of you is elder?"

"Kelly is elder by a minute," I say.

"How old are you now?"

"Twelve," I say.

"Anything you have to say to your parents?" She asks, "Are they anywhere in the crowd?"

Of course, they aren't! My mother is dead. My father never bothered to look for us or take care of us after her death. I felt like telling that to her, but it would ruin my birthday.

"I came with my friends," I say, trying to keep up my smile as my heart sobs.

"Wow! That's nice," she says. "Now, who wants some music? Let's give it up for the rapper… Roger Smith! And the beatboxer… Jake Johnson!"

The crowd cheers loudly.

Kelly and I get off the stage and back to the table with Fenna. I hear some beatboxing sounds from backstage. Two men with jet-black and spiked hair emerge. One of them is beatboxing. The other starts to rap. He starts off with a soft tune and then goes into intense rapping. He sings more songs. The beat builds lively enthusiasm in the crowd. My smile widens by the second. I grab some food and start talking to Fenna. Turns out, the whole team had planned this party.

I decide to join the people dancing on the stage. Some go for extreme dancing: backflips, aerials, split jumps, cartwheels, etc. Some go for style dancing: slide to the right, spin on one leg, etc. Some go for fun dancing: clumsily moving legs, jumping around, etc. Fenna and I go for fun dancing.

I spot Franz, Azteque, and Davian trying to copy the guys doing cool dance moves. Alassia tries to pull Kelly towards the stage, but she is too shy to join.

The day goes on like that. Dancing. Singing — a few kids got to sing on the mic. Partying.

Once the party was over, late at night, everyone started to leave. Soon, there was no one left except Master Ed, the team, and me. *Why do I feel like someone is missing?*

I blink out of that thought as Master Ed wishes me.

"Happy Birthday, Danica and Kelly," he says while handing us a gift box.

"Oooh! What's inside?" I ask a bit too greedily.

"Guess!"

"Err… I've finally gotten a cool fighting suit?"

"Not worth a birthday gift from six magical friends," Franz says.

"Is it a magical fighting suit?"

"Is a fighting suit all you like?"

"They're cool!"

"Just open up your gift!"

"Sure!"

I tear through the wrapper to unbox my gift. When I open it, I see the lamest thing ever! Shoes.

"Nice gift! I thought shoes aren't worth a birthday gift from six magical friends," I say.

"Ordinary shoes aren't worth it. But, are these ordinary? Do you really think we'd give a lame — I mean nice — friend, ordinary shoes?" Franz looks a bit offended.

"Then what is this?"

"Shoes..."

"Lame!"

"That can hover underwater, smoke the place so that you can make a shadow exit — Poof! — I thought up that shadow exit thingy, by the way."

"Now, I am listening!"

"It can speed you up, and it can change colour according to your emotion. Kelly also got the same thing," Franz says.

I wear the shoes to test them out. The shoes are very soft and comfy on the inside. I run towards the lake around the camp. As I run, I realise an increase in my speed. As if the shoes were giving me a boost. I notice that they turn from pearl white to daffodil yellow. I dive into the lake. When I stop kicking, deep underwater, I end up floating. I realise that this isn't because of my powers because I never float underwater. Is it the shoes? I look at my shoes again, and they are celeste blue. These are so cool!

I get out of the water, and the shoes dry away instantly. I head back to the tents. Everyone is sitting around the campfire. I go and have a seat with the rest.

"Hi, birthday girl! We were just putting in ideas on how we can whack that immortal crazy dude," Franz says. "I say Alassia could just shape-shift him into an ant. Poof, he's harmless!"

"I told you I've not mastered shape-shifting heavy objects into lighter ones," Alassia complains.

"Master Ed could do it," he says.

"He will still be able to give orders to his people and accomplish his cruel goals in different ways. Also, I am supposed to protect you all, not go about turning people into ants. Evil or not," Master Ed says.

"Got any better ideas?"

"As a matter of fact, I do. You guys know the Revenir mole? The mole opposite your elbow," Master Ed says. "As a guardian, I will need to touch that so he can get out of this Revenir spirit, and stay alive without remembering anything about his powers or the Revenirs."

"Why didn't you ever do that?" Franz complains.

"It isn't as easy as you think. He's got skills! I tried once and ended up coming on the news."

"So, you were the masked man? No wonder I felt a strange connection with you," I say.

"Maybe I have an idea!" Kelly exclaims, inviting all eyes towards her. "Danica could use her powers to freeze Zephyr, and then Master Ed could touch the mole."

"Good idea," Master Ed says.

"Only one problem," Fenna says.

"Go on."

"We don't know which of his many lairs he is in. It'll take years to find him. Though that'll give quite enough time to Danica to practise with ice," Fenna adds.

"How about, Master Ed time-travel himself and take Danica along to the last time he was seen," Davian suggests.

"…which was on the news!"

"Yes!"

"Well, that means I've got some practising to do," I say.

I smile and head back to the lake again. If I'm going to master ice, I must practise more.

Again, I summon water. This time, I feel more confident. I know the trick. I touch the water with both my hands. I will the water to turn into ice. I close my eyes, focusing on my emotions. I put all my emotions into it. Even the faintest ones. My happiness (for having such a great birthday party), my anger (at Zephyr for ruining a perfect day at the water park), my sorrow (because of my mother's death), and many more countless emotions.

I feel something cold in my hand. But, this time, it feels different. The cold feeling travels from my hand to my shoulder, chest, stomach, thighs, knees, calves, ankles, heels, and toes. From my shoulders, it goes up to my neck, chin, mouth, and nose. When it comes to my eyes, I realise what's up. My whole body is ice!

I try jumping to get help. Dumb idea. I try to balance, which is very difficult, covered in ice. I jump again, trying to balance while landing. I jump a third time. This time, the ice had enough of me jumping. I fall onto my stomach. Lucky for me, the ice secured my fall, or else my stomach and nose would be flat.

After two minutes of being coated with ice, my body starts to freeze. Not the kind of freezing that happens in the most extreme cold of snow. Even worse. It's like the continent Before the Bomb Era (BBE) that people used to call Antarctica. It was the era before the world exploded, when places like France, India, and the United States existed over ten milleniums ago.

I was shivering badly, but the ice makes sure I don't move a muscle. Even breathing isn't easy, but I manage to keep it up.

Since I was laying on my stomach because of the fall, I decide to sleep. When I wake up, it's the next morning. The sun is shining brightly. The only problem is, the sun can't melt the ice that I form. I try rolling around. Kind of like how you do on a hill. But, I can't. During the night, the ice stuck itself to the ground. Now, this is a whole lot better! Great.

It would have been helpful if the others came to check in on me. But, since no one came looking for me the whole night and hours of the morning, I realise I need to figure out how to get rid of this ice on my own.

If Kelly was here, she would say something like *'Use your powers, dummy!'*

I haven't mastered turning water into ice. Forget about turning ice to water without even being able to move my hand. Still, it's worth a try. I repeat the process once again. At first, nothing happens. But then, I felt water dripping down my hand. The ice was melting. Slowly, the ice all over my body starts melting, until I am completely dripping wet. Though the ice has vanished, my hands and the rest of my body is still freezing.

I shiver as I walk back to the tents. When I reach, I see no one. I check the dark forest, and there they are. They are practising their powers.

Alassia is nowhere to be seen. Instead, there is a 43 kg twig lying around. Davian keeps disappearing and reappearing with pictures of the ancient and future world. Kelly was drawing on a… leaf? It must be my eyes playing tricks on me. I rub my eyes. Still a leaf! Fenna is zapping some targets. Franz seems to be trying to check what's going on in his house. Apparently, his parents have worried expressions on their faces, while talking to the police.

"Mom and Dad are so worried, still. After two years!" He looks glum.

House. Suddenly something appears in my mind. How could I be so careless? Forgetting the two annoying brothers I have!

"Hey, Franz! Do you think you could try searching for my two brothers?"

"Huh?" He comes back out of his supervision. "Uh, yeah sure."

He gets back into the supervision zone again, hopefully searching for my brothers this time.

Suddenly, someone appears right in front of me. Unlucky for that guy who appeared out of nowhere, I have reflexes. Real bad ones. I gesture a punch and the water from the lake nearby pushes him.

"Azteque!" I whine when I take a good look at the guy. "Next time try not to appear right in front of someone. Are you okay?"

"Not a bit. I never knew water can be so harsh."

"There is something I always knew. That you're a little annoying guy," I say, though I don't sound annoyed.

"Guess what I just saw!"

"What?"

"The Wind Cheetahs beat the Leopards at the finals of the Magball tournament this year!" Azteque exclaims.

"Garrett Denzel for the win! Wooh!"

"Who is Carrot Dansil?" Kelly asks.

"Garrett Denzel! G-A-R-R-E-T-T space D-E-N-Z-E-L," I spell.

"Only the former captain of the Wind Cheetahs and the most famous player in Magball history," Fenna comes in.

"The former captain of cheetahs? So, the most famous player is a cheetah?" She wonders.

"Since when have you gotten so dumb, dummy?"

"I haven't gotten dumb. I'm thinking you're dumb enough to say that a cheetah, whose name is 'Carrot', is the most famous player in Magball history!"

I roll my eyes. "Forget it. There is no point explaining to you about Magball."

I turn to Azteque, "So, Az, tell me exactly how the match went. Every single detail! Don't miss even a millisecond of the match, got it?"

"Sure!"

He tells me about the whole match — the part when the Wind Cheetahs score their first goal, when the Leopards block the Wind Cheetah's second goal, when the Wind Cheetahs snatch a ball from one of the Leopards' hands, and so on…

In case you didn't know, Magball is a sport played with magnetic balls in a magnetic field. There are two sets of ten balls. The colour of the balls depends on the colour of each team. In the Wind Cheetahs vs. Leopards match, the balls for the Wind Cheetahs were yellow and that for the Leopards were orange.

There are aim boards. Four on each side. Each aim board is a different colour and size. The red one is the smallest and is worth 200 points; it is 30 feet high. The green one is the second smallest and is worth 150 points; it is 25 feet high. The blue one is the second largest and is worth 100 points; it is 20 feet high. The yellow one is the largest and is worth only 50 points; it is 15 feet high. The winner isn't the one who finishes first (even though the game gets over at that point) but is the one who has the most points once a team has finished.

Oh, and the coolest thing in Magball is that we don't play on foot; we play on hoverboards. They are circular and the colour painted on them is the colour of your team.

Another cool thing is that the balls are magnetic, so they stick to the board. Though scoring may sound easy, it's not. There is one player on each side — the defender — who stops the ball from scoring. There are five runners who do the passing, catching, and scoring part. There is one snatcher who pushes the ball out of the opponent's hands.

Once Azteque is done explaining all the match details to me, I go on to practise my water skills. I dive into the water with the shoes I got for my birthday. Once underwater, I spin around. Faster. Faster. The shoes are a great help. Soon, I have created a mini tornado. I keep spinning to keep up with the tornado. After a few minutes of spinning, my head feels dizzy. My body feels tired. So, I stop. Panting, I gesture for the water to spit me out of the lake. I lie down on the ground. When I look around, everyone seems wet.

"Whoopsies," I say.

"Danica! Get this water off me," they all whine.

"Sorry, too tired, can't!"

"Come on!"

"Okay, okay! I was just kidding." I gesture for the water on them to come towards me and go back into the lake. "Is that fine now?"

Suddenly, Franz wakes up from his sightseeing.

"Guys, I think Lez is captured. No wait, Zeph is sharing his plans with her. Do you think…?"

"Oh, I do. I-M-P-O-S-T-E-R," I spell. "That explains why she wasn't at the end of the party."

"It also explains why she wanted to have the party. It was a distraction," Alassia suggests.

"It also explains a part of the prophecy. *You will be betrayed by a teammate.* That is Lezabel," I add.

"Oh no, you guys! We must cancel the time-travel-and-freeze-mister-scar-face plan. Lezabel knows about it, and she might be telling it to Zephyr," Kelly adds.

"I froze in ice for nothing?"

"Now what? Plan B? What is our backup plan?" Fenna asks.

"Uhh… I dunno," Franz says.

"Did you find my brothers?" I ask him.

"No, I tried searching but I don't know what they look like. So, it will be harder to look for them, especially if they are far from here."

I give him a sad nod.

Franz concentrates again.

"Wait a second, Lezabel is coming back. I'll spy on her to see where Zeph is hiding," he suggests.

"Good idea!"

"And, we'll just continue practising. Hey, Fenna, wanna fight?" I ask.

"Game on!"

"I am so gonna beat you," I challenge.

"We'll see."

Fenna electrocutes her hands and zaps the lightning at me. I quickly summon a water bubble and shield myself from the attack. I gesture a punch and the water smashes Fenna or was supposed to, but instead, Fenna runs aside, dodging my attack. She throws back a strike of lightning. Too late, I summon water, but it's too late. The zap hits me right in the stomach. I fall on my back. My stomach pains badly. I use up all my remaining strength to summon some water to heal my stomach. The cold water kills the pain.

"I did just beat you," Fenna says.

"Great job!"

"Thank you, water girl! I truly am the best, aren't I?"

"Don't push it." I smile.

-10-

Enemy Territory

Suddenly, Franz blinks out of spying. "Guys! I figured out where Zephyr is hiding. In the Tenebris Forest. This time, he isn't in a tree; he is under fake soil."

"It'll take years searching for fake soil in the largest forest on Earth," I say.

"I know the almost exact location of the place. Let's teleport there." Franz turns to Azteque.

"Not a good idea. I'm still not good at teleporting more than two people. We could have been hurt last time if not for Master Ed," Davian says.

"Master Ed?" We ask.

"If you're going to fight a war, you have got to figure things out by yourselves," he demands.

"War?" we ask.

"*A big battle will come by,*" he quotes the prophecy. "Remember?"

"Right," I say.

"I could shapeshift to a Pegasus and give you guys a ride," Alassia suggests.

"Good idea," Azteque says.

"Quick, Lezabel is about to come back," Franz states.

Alassia turns into a white Pegasus. Her wings spread wide. My Pegasus, Flake, looks way smaller than her, and he is plain white. Alassia has what looks like freckles all over her.

"Perfect," I say.

I hop onto Alassia — the Pegasus. Everyone else does too. Alassia takes off, and we soar through the sky.

"I always wanted to travel the world. And now, here we are, travelling! We've visited Auberfort, stayed there for two years, and now we're visiting Colzieu. This trip would have rocked if we weren't just flying to enemy territory," I say.

"By the way, what's the plan? Why exactly are we going there? To touch Zephyr's mole? To capture him? To do what?" Kelly asks.

"I've got an idea. So, here's the plan," Franz says.

He starts briefing us on the plan. Unexpected of him, the plan does make sense and is perfect.

"Alassia, you heard that, right?" I ask the Pegasus.

"Yup!" she replies.

Wait a second, did the Pegasus just talk?

"Ahh!" We all scream, slightly jumping into the air.

"Relax! I can talk even if I am a wooden stick. You wanna see?" she asks.

"No! No, no, no!"

Too late. The Pegasus already turned into a wooden stick. We all start falling.

"Whoops, not what I had in mind," Alassia apologises.

"Davian, your watch!" I tell Davian as we continue falling.

He nods, understanding what I mean. He looks at his watch and changes the time to five minutes ago.

"Yup!" Alassia says.

Davian had successfully re-winded the time to right before Alassia's shapeshift. This time, after Alassia speaks, no one screams.

"Alassia, next time try to take into account who is sitting on you!"

"Sorry!" she apologises again.

"I'm gonna sleep." I yawn.

"Same!"

"Me too!"

"What about me? I don't have an auto-drive option," Alassia complains.

By the time she is done with her sentence, we are all snoring.

"Guys! Wake up! We're about to reach," Alassia yells.

"We're awake," I say. Or maybe half-awake.

After about five minutes, we reach.

"Here is where Plan A starts. Danica and I will go in from here. Alassia will fly with Kelly to the northern entrance. Azteque and Fenna will teleport to the southern entrance. Davian and Master Ed will teleport to the eastern entrance. We know what to do from there," Franz says.

We all get to our positions.

Franz puts his hand in the soil. He moves it around as if to find something in it.

"Aha!" he exclaims as he pulls a lever to reveal a tunnel. I was about to go in when he says, "Wait. Security. This is a sneaky mission. No fighting. I've got an idea."

As the guard turns around, I send water at him. The water turned to ice, as I had hoped, freezing the guard. We quickly go down the tunnel. The whole place is a metal corridor. We make turns, freezing guards on the way. Everything is going as planned. Suddenly, I hear someone speak.

"Guys, Master Ed and I are at the cameras. Can you hear us?" Comes the voice of Davian.

"Yes, we can. Try to whisper, though. Don't wanna attract attention," I say.

"We passed a few guards, but Master Ed managed to mess with their minds. Azteque is going to switch positions with Master Ed in 3... 2... 1... now I've Azteque with me," Davian says.

"Okay, everything going as planned till now?" Franz asks.

"Luck is with us, till now!" Davian says.

"We better get going," Franz says.

Franz and I keep walking. That's when we see the first room in the lair. The room has a key card opening. It would have been better if it were a passcode. Franz could look around the place to figure it out.

"The guards. They'd be having the key card or a master card," I suggest.

"Great idea!"

We retrace our steps to find the last guard I froze. I unfreeze the part of the ice that had a master card. I snatch it and quickly freeze him again. Now, I have gotten quite fluent in freezing and unfreezing.

We go back to the room. I press the master card to the biometrics device. Bingo! A green light flashes on the device, and the room opens quickly. Franz and I quickly hide behind both sides of the door. We take a small peek. No one. The coast is clear. We go into the room, and the door slams shut behind us. The room is filled with files, poisons, and potions.

"Hey, Azteque," Franz says to the CCTV camera. "Do you mind teleporting all these potions to the underground hole that Danica is digging right now?"

"Sure!"

I use the water in the soil to dig a hole underground, right in front of the entrance we came from. Everything in the room, except for the furniture, is wiped out and seemingly placed in the hole I made. I make the hole way larger, probably fifty times the size of the room, just so we can fit everything in it. Then, I cover the hole with soil, just so no one sees it.

"I'll take a few pictures of this room." Franz blinks every time he turns his head and finally says, "Done!"

"Okay then, come on. We'll finish nothing if we keep up this speed!"

We go out of the room. According to the plan, Alassia and Kelly should be in the air vents, spying on a meeting of the people who fight for Zephyr. Master Ed would be teleporting all the goods in the meeting room to the same hole I made. Fenna and Master Ed should be in the control center, shooting lightning at the systems to destroy them.

"If we wanna go faster, let's split up. You take the room on the right, and I'll take the one on the left. Meet up, in this corridor," I suggest.

Franz nods.

Before I go to the room on the left, I open the right one with the master card, so that Franz can go in.

"Azteque, this room?"

"On it!" Azteque teleports the spheres.

We keep checking rooms until Franz is pretty sure we are done with all. At this point, Kelly and Alassia are meant to be waiting in the air vents in the room that Zephyr is in. Franz and I go to the air vents and reach Alassia and Kelly. We make sure not to make a sound.

I look out of the air vent and see two men. One is an agile-looking man with sand skin. He has sunset hair neatly styled in a modern quiff haircut. He doesn't have a beard or moustache. His eyes are plain ash grey. The man's teeth are gapped and crooked, and his nose is beaky. He has a scowling look. His voice is crackling.

Seeing him up close, I realise who this guy is — Zephyr. The other man looks oddly familiar. He has the same voice, the same red hair… Dad? What is he doing here? Is he captured? If he is, I am going out right now and kicking that immortal man to his death (which, I just realised, is impossible). I can't let another part of my family die.

I listen to them talking closely.

"You have killed your wife; what is the problem in killing your sons? The more vulnerable Kelly and Danica are, the easier for me to get them," Zephyr calmly tells my dad.

WHAT! I can't believe my ears. Dad killed Mom? Dad works for Zephyr? My anger burns. I feel like getting out of the vent and blasting water at my dad.

After Zephyr is defeated, if we ever can, I am gonna have a quick, calm word with you, Dad! I mutter to myself. The second line of the prophecy makes sense now! *The one you love will be someone you truly hate.* I loved Dad, but now I truly hate him.

"You will get yourself killed if you refuse to do it. You have seen me fight before, haven't you?" Zephyr threatens.

"Okay, I'll do it. Just spare me," Dad says with fear in his eyes.

Oh no! Dad is going to kill my brothers. I've got to save them. I eye Kelly. She gives me a look as if saying, *I am so gonna kill Dad.*

Dad leaves the room, probably preparing for the kill.

Right now, as per the plan, Fenna and Master Ed should be freeing all the prisoners and leading them outside the lair.

"Yes, Drake?" Zephyr asks in his regular cold voice, as a man, Drake (the guy who chased me after I returned from the dead), steps in.

"All the guards are frozen. The prisoner cells are empty. The rooms have nothing but furniture. All potions, poisons, bots, files, computers… everything has disappeared. The control system has malfunctioned. Nothing is working. The security room door has been frozen; none of us is able to get in," Drake states in a worried tone.

"Search every inch of this place. Whoever has done this shall be captured, immediately," Zephyr says, in a weird, cold voice with burning-hot anger.

Drakes rushes out of the room.

Suddenly, everything gets wiped out from Zephyr's room. When I look at Master Ed, he winks.

Zephyr seems to be shocked. "How come? Never in my life have things disappeared here!"

Alassia turns into a spider — an extremely disgusting spider. She crawls out of the vent and into Zephyr's room. She tries to bug Zephyr and crawls on him. No luck. Instead, Zephyr ends up crushing her. Yuck. Disgusting. If Alassia is a spider, does that mean she is dead?

Suddenly, Alassia is back in the vent with not a scratch. Davian must have re-winded time. This time she turns into a fly. Same process. She gets crushed. Davian rewinds. She turns into another animal and goes through the same thing.

Finally, she thinks up something clever. She turns into Drake. She starts moving out of the vent. She tries to make no noise, but she sadly does. We all, except Alassia/Drake, shuffle towards an edge and hide there. Zephyr opens the vent. He sees Alassia/Drake.

"Drake, what are you doing here?"

"Just checking if anyone is here, Sir. No one, it seems." Somehow, Alassia changed her voice to match Drake's.

"Okay, then get on with it."

"Yes, Sir!"

Zephyr closes the vent and turns around, trying to find as many files as he can. Of course, thanks to Master Ed, he finds none.

Alassia/Drake goes out of the vent. Soon, she enters from the door of Zephyr's room.

"What is it, Drake?" Zephyr asks.

"I've searched every inch of this place. No footstep. No fingerprints. Nothing at all," Alassia/Drake says.

"Have you checked outside the lair? They might have escaped."

"I saw many footsteps over there, but they have a dead end. I'm guessing they flew to wherever they were going," Alassia/Drake lies.

"Take the fighters to find them. I'm guessing these pests are stupid Revenirs and that Eddie guy. Ask any guard who is not frozen to break the ice off the frozen ones," Zephyr orders.

"There aren't any unfro—" She never got to finish her sentence because in came the last person we wanted to see.

"Sir, we've found a few fingerpri… Is that me?" the real Drake asks.

"Is that me?" Alassia/Drake tries to continue pretending.

"Which one of you is Drake?" Zephyr asks alarmed.

Both raise their hands.

"Which one of you is a liar?"

Both point at each other.

"Which one of you loves spears?"

Alassia/Drake raises her hand.

"Sad for you, you're wrong, fake Drake," he says to Alassia-Drake as she transforms back to Alassia.

"I suppose I tricked you for a few seconds. It was too easy," she says, full of sarcasm. "Who knows what I could have done if this brat hadn't come in."

She keeps commenting, trying to stall, while I slowly throw my boomerang out of the vent. It goes towards Zephyr and is about to hit him, but his senses are too good. He ducks right in time and snatches the boomerang from the air as if it were the easiest attack he has ever experienced.

"Is there anything easier than that?" Zephyr asks. Suddenly, he falls to the ground.

"I'm pretty sure it's not the punch I just did," Alassia says.

Zephyr gets up. After that, everything happens a little too quickly... Zephyr takes out his sword and strikes Alassia. She ends up bleeding on her right arm. Yet, she bravely stands up. She shapeshifts into an elephant and swirls her trunk around Zephyr. Zephyr struggles. She raises Zephyr and slams him to the floor. Then, she turns into a lion.

"I am not scared of lions. They can't kill me. I am immortal!" Zephyr grins.

She roars in Zephyr's face. He gets pushed backwards and slammed onto the wall.

She turns into water this time, clearly for me to use. I control the water and turn it into ice. A long thin stick of ice with both sharp ends. I jump down the vent, take the ice, and use it like a blade. The only funny thing about it is that I am about to kill the scarface with Alassia being my sword.

I throw Alassia/Sword towards Zephyr. As expected, he dodges. However, that was too predictable. Davian had thought it up too well. He seemed to have slowed down Zephyr and speeded Alassia, the Ice Sword. That made Zephyr's dodging way slower and Alassia/Sword could hit him just in time. For some reason, she, all of a sudden, turns into a baseball bat, and Zephyr gets hit with the bat instead. Why she turned into a bat, I do not know. The speed goes back to normal. Zephyr falls to the ground at normal speed, though it would have looked funny in Slow-Mo. Alassia turns into an eagle before she could fall, flies next to me, and turns back to her human form.

"Why did you turn into a baseball bat?" I ask.

"I dunno. First, I am a sword, and the next second, I am shapeshifting into a baseball bat. Then I thought it best to stop transforming. But again, I start transforming. It's like my mind was conflicting with my powers."

"It was more like Ed and I were fighting!" A girl's voice comes in. Lezabel. At first, I was confused, but then I realised what was going on. She must've been controlling Alassia's mind and Master Ed probably tried to stop her.

"Please, imposter brain, could you be smarter? You could have made her turn into water. The baseball bat hit your dear friend," I say.

I try hiding my fear.Deep down though, I am utterly terrified (hopefully, she doesn't notice that). We have got to fight an immortal scarface and a mind-reading imposter brain.

Lezabel gives a look saying, *Why did I not think of that?* But then, she washes it off.

-11-

Jailbreak

"You have figured it out, I see. Yes, I'm the imposter," Lezabel says.

"Not too hard. Did you think we wouldn't realise if one of us was missing? You're not as smart as we thought you are. You do know that you could have used mind tricks on us so we'd never figure it out, right?" Kelly says while jumping out of the vent, followed by everyone else.

"Eddie deary wouldn't have gotten influenced. Instead, he'd become more cautious," bat-brain Lezabel states.

"I like Ed better. Eddie doesn't suit me, forget about 'deary'," Master Ed complains.

Suddenly, Zephyr gets up. Scowling, he puts up his middle and index fingers in both hands and joins them, like how Fenna does to strike lightning. He looks like he's getting ready for combat. Oh wait, he is.

"I'm guessing it's combat time," Fenna says.

"I'm starting to hate that scarface," Davian says as he and Azteque appear out of nowhere.

"I'm starting to hate that bat-brain," Azteque says looking at Lezabel.

"I'm starting to hate both," I say.

"Master Ed, deflect all the mind control from Lezabel," I demand.

"Sure," Master Ed says.

"Kelly, we need a few origami animals," I say.

She nods and starts drawing.

"Davian, slow their attacks and dodges, and make us faster," I suggest. "Alassia, a dragon would be good to fight this immortal scarface!"

She nods and shapeshifts into a green dragon, probably ten times taller than the tallest human. She doesn't fit, but she manages to lean down quite enough.

"The rest, fight," I say.

"It's a cakewalk," Franz says and attacks.

"I've got some soil controlling to do," I say.

I crack my knuckles to use the water in the soil under the metal room. I make the soil push a part of the metal, where Lezabel and the scarface are standing. It makes them jump up into the sky and land on their knees.

If I'm lucky, they might as well land on their head. Sadly, I'm not lucky. I try to distract them as much as I can, so the others can attack more easily. Suddenly, I get an idea. It would either work, or get us all killed. Then, Zephyr will laugh at our faces. But, it's worth a try.

"Guys, we just need the scarface fallen down! Then Master Ed can take it from there," I state.

Suddenly, Zephyr does the last thing I expected him to do. Out of his two fingers that were put up, he summons something black. It looks more like black lightning. I guess exactly what it is. Death. Zephyr summons it towards me. I can't move because of shock. The strike almost hits me.

But then, something weird happens. I feel nothing. No pain. No death. I open my eyes. Master Ed has fallen, looking so weak. But surely, he isn't dead. He can't be; he is an immortal man. He must have come in front of me to save me from getting hurt.

"What was the point of that?" Kelly booms. "What is the point of all this wickedness?"

"Obviously, power!" Zephyr scoffs.

"Why do you care so much about power?"

"Power symbolises strength."

"Vileness destroys reputation."

"You children wouldn't get it. You're just twelve. I am 200."

"Quam bene vivas refert non quam diu," she says. "It is how well you live that matters, not how long.'"

"I don't care about stupid Greek phrases."

"Latin."

"My point, dear, is that power is the one most important thing in life."

"Nothing is as important as being a noble person. A kind person. Not a wicked character like you," Kelly says.

"Why, Kayla —"

"Kelly," she interrupts.

"Whatever!" He bellows. "Why, Kelly, would I listen to a stubborn, annoyingly clever girl like you?"

"I don't care if you listen to me or not. I am simply playing my part by trying to make you realise that what you're doing is making others' lives unfortunate. Would you like to make peoples' lives melancholic just for your sake? Would you?"

"If it means I will get what I want, sure!"

"You will never understand, will you?"

"Alassia, water," I say, while Kelly is debating with Zephyr.

Alassia quickly shapeshifts into water. I turn the water cold and splash it onto Master Ed. It starts to heal him. He gets more energy by the minute.

"Be careful of his death strike. One shot and you're dead," he says.

"This dude is getting more impossible by the minute," I say.

"We'll need to escape. We can't stay here, or we're bound to get shot," Master Ed says.

"We could use the vent," I say.

"But, the vent is too high."

"That means it's time to control soil."

"Look out," Fenna says as Zephyr shoots another death strike at Alassia.

Alassia dodges.

I quickly make the soil push the metal upwards to form a mini metal mountain. We quickly climb up the mountain and start making our way up to the vent. Of course, in the process, we dodge many death strikes, but we reach the top. Then, I block the entrance with water that Kelly draws quickly.

"Let's go! It's only a matter of time before they catch us," I say.

"Alassia, is it possible for you to shapeshift us?" Kelly asks.

"Clever idea! Though, I've never tried it."

"Now is your chance," Davian says.

"I'll try, just don't complain if it hurts in the process." Alassia agrees.

She focuses on one of us at a time. First, she goes with Kelly. She focuses hard. Suddenly, Kelly disappears. No wait, she's a teeny-weeny ant who weighs 43 kg. Then, she does me. My muscles tingle and then they pain badly. In less than a millisecond, Alassia is the size of a giant. I jump. Ahh!

"Relax! We're ants," says the ant next to me. "By the way, I'm Kelly."

"I realised. Your voice is the same."

Soon enough, we all are ants.

"Isn't it gonna take years to reach outside?" I ask.

"Not if I speed us up." Davian winks.

He looks at his minuscule watch. We continue walking. Suddenly, we are walking so fast, we are probably the world's fastest ants! I can barely see my legs. After a minute or so, we are out of the vent. We continue running. Suddenly, a huge footstep is close to stepping on us. We quickly run aside and dodge the step. When the man moves on, we realise that was Zephyr.

After five minutes of running, we take a short break. I summon water from a bottle five meters away, and we start drinking. One nano-droplet of water is a whole glass full of water for ants. We continue moving.

It looks like we are in a giant's lair. Humans look more like scary beasts. The chairs look like huge thrones. The tables look more like enormous man-made caves. Phones look like huge TVs lying around. Mini statues, that people normally have in their houses, look more like huge tourist attractions. The paper looks like an enormous carpet. One key on a keyboard is more like a big button you are meant to jump on.

After another five minutes, we reach the entrance. Alassia turns us back into normal-sized people. Bad idea. Drake was guarding the entrance. Everything happens in the blink of an eye. He smokes the place and captures us. Even Franz and Master Ed couldn't see through it. It must be some potion that we hadn't spotted.

Suddenly, we find ourselves in a cellar, in a metal room, which is securely locked. Even Master Ed struggles badly. He looks exhausted. Must be the effect of the death strike.

"Guys, I am going to give you immortality. Let me touch your moles," Master Ed says.

"Really?" I ask, surprised.

"Why?" Alassia asks.

"Just so you don't get affected by the death strike, of course," he states.

"Yaaaay," we exclaim.

Master Ed hesitates. He exhales as if he's getting ready to step into his doomsday party.

"One by one, I'll touch your moles," he says. "If I hand you immortality, I am giving you a part of mine. If I give it to all of you equally, I won't have it anymore. If I die, please fulfil a few wishes of mine. One of you shall become the new guardian. Got it?"

"No! Are you crazy? Death isn't quite fun. You have to keep your immortality," I say.

"I've lived long enough. However bad death might be, I don't mind. If I die, I will die a martyr. So, I won't go into eternal darkness as you did. Don't worry, child!"

Everyone's faces turn to me.

"You have experienced death?" They all ask, their eyes widened.

"Yeah! Worst experience."

"Tell us everything!" They demand. I tell them everything from the top.

Once I am done, everyone is amazed at how brave I am. They were all hugging me one after the other when Master Ed interrupted.

"Great job, Danica! Now, everyone, show me your hands."

Once he is done giving all of us immortality, he looks weak. All the colour has drained away from his face.

"Master Ed," I ask, "are you okay?"

"I am no more your guardian but merely a fellow fighter. But, ah, yes, I am fine," he ensures.

Though he doesn't look fine.

"Can I call you Eddie-Dums?" Davian asks.

"Or… how would this sound?" Alassia clears her throat. She pretends to hold the tip of an imaginary hat. "Bonjour, Master Edward Revenir! I've heard 'Revenir' is French for 'come-back'," she says in a French accent.

"Did you Google Translate that?" Master Ed says.

"Goggles Translate? What on earth do you mean by that?" Franz asks.

"BBE thing. Never mind," Master Ed says.

"Guys, focus. We need to talk jailbreak," Franz says.

"Franz has got a point! We should try and figure out how to get out of here," says Kelly.

"Would you like to try teleporting us? Who knows if it will work?" I ask Azteque.

"I can't," he says.

"Aww, come on, man! Of course, you can." I encourage him.

"I literally can't. There is something blocking my powers from working properly."

"Oh!"

"Guys, I think I see some sort of a purple gooey liquid covering the walls. You guys won't be able to see it. I can only see it with my powers." Franz says.

"Like paint?"

"Kind of. But there are also some sort of black dots in it. Something like powder."

"He of all people has actually figured it out," Master Ed says.

"Figured what?" I ask.

"That potion is a mixture of minuscule parts of Lezabel and Zephyr's power. If two people combine their powers, they get a powerful potion that they could achieve anything with," he says.

"We could combine our powers to make a potion that could break us out of here," I suggest.

"That takes time and no disturbance," Master Ed says.

"We've quite enough time. Kelly, water!" I say.

She quickly unfolds her drawing tool, the ninja star and sketches something on the wall of the prison. She swipes it out.

Soon there is a puddle of water. I control the water to make an ice barrier so no one can disturb us.

"Now, we can do it. Err… how do we do it?" I ask.

All eyes turn to our ex-guardian.

"Are you sure you want to? It requires a lot of strength."

"We're sure!"

"You also need to be prepa—" he says.

"Tell us how to do it," we yell, maybe a little too loud.

"Okay. But, just in case —" He stops when he sees our scowls. "Okay, okay. First, you need to focus on your powers. Fenna and Danica…" He looks at us.

"Yes?"

"Focus on your powers. Water…" He looks at me. "Lightning…" He turns to Fenna.

"What if there isn't any water to focus on?" Then I notice the ice. "Never mind."

I lock my eyes on the ice and focus on it. At least I try to. There is still something in the back of my mind bothering me. Dad would probably be hunting for our brothers right now. He would have probably already gained their trust. Though, our brothers aren't gullible. They wouldn't just go to our dad and tell him, *We still love you, Dad, even after you left us alone when Mom died!*

Nope. Not something they would say. There isn't much time until Dad kills them,which means I need to get out of here as soon as possible. I need to make that pellet. I need to focus. *So, focus, Danica!*

I focus on the water. Focus hard. But then, sadly, the focus is broken when Davian asks, "Uh, what next? After focusing?"

"Now, when you're completely focused on your power, use it. Danica, control water. Make the biggest water tornado you can."

"Not to interrupt, but how on earth is she supposed to control water without breaking the barrier?" Franz asks the question I have in my mind.

"I got that under control! I mean, not the water under my control, but I can get more water for her." Kelly draws water and spills it on the floor. "There you go!"

"And, Fenna, electrocute yourself," Master Ed demands.

I control the water on the floor. I twirl like a ballerina. Soon, I feel myself lifting off the ground. My eyes are sealed tight. I keep spinning in the air. How big my tornado is, I don't know. I feel so dizzy, I almost stop, until I realise I mustn't. I keep twirling. Sweat trickles down my face. I use the sweat to make the tornado go faster.

I slowly open my eyes to take a sneak-peak at Fenna. She is electrocuted, but she isn't twitching. She is levitating in the sky about as high as I am. Man, sometimes I feel jealous of that girl's powers.

"Now, you both come towards each other. When you reach the middle point, pass through each other and to the other end. Got it?" Master Ed says.

Weird. As far as I can remember, I am not a ghost! I keep going forward. When we are close to each other, I hesitate. What if I am too bad at this and I just bump into her and then fall and humiliate myself? But then, the thought of my brothers came to me. I must go forward. I just keep walking — more like levi-walking (levitating plus walking) — and before I know it, I'm on the other end.

"Now," Master Ed says, "you both can come back down."

I slow down and descend. The second I touch the floor, I black out.

I open my eyes five hours later.

"What," I start. "What happened? Is the pellet made?"

Kelly nods. She holds out a pellet of the colour blue.

"We need to burst out quick," I say, urgently.

Every second counts. At any minute now, my dad would raise a sword at my brothers.

"Alassia is working on it," Kelly points.

"Where did she get the potion ingredients from?" I ask.

"Me," Kelly says.

"Oh, right!"

"Bingo!" Alassia exclaims, "Made the potion. It is as thick as paint."

"Perfect!" Master Ed says. "Kelly, we will need a paintbrush!"

"There you go." She throws him a paintbrush.

Master Ed dips the paintbrush into the potion. Then, he uses the paintbrush to paint on top of the potion Zephyr and Lezabel made. Two minutes later, the good potion kills the evil potion and allows us to go out. Alassia turns us into ants, again. Davian speeds us up, once more. We run out of the hideout. As expected, there is a guard at the door.

This time, we don't turn into human form just yet. We first go towards the trees. Then, Alassia turns us into lions. The guard turns. He sees us. His expression turns from savage to fearful. We all come out and roar.

"Ahh!" he screams.

Then, he does the cleverest thing. He slowly opens the entrance and gets inside as quickly as ever.

Suddenly, I turn back to my human form.

We all laugh at the guard. Then, Alassia turns into a Pegasus.

"Hop on," she says.

We go on a peaceful ride to some place in Colzieu. It would be better if we were around the same place as Zephyr, then we wouldn't have to take 10 hours of rides to his secret headquarters.

"What happened to the potions, files, poisons, etc?" I ask Azteque.

"I've sent it to the ocean on the other side of the world. We can dispose them when we land," Azteque says.

"Where exactly are we landing?" I ask.

"Mount Magna, the mountains in Oscia," she says.

-12-

Brother Hunt

The knee-deep snow glows in the moonlight. The relaxing wind pushes my hair to my left. Suddenly, I feel a smack on my face.

"Ow!"

"Ha!" Franz says with an evil grin on his face.

"For the ten-millionth time, do not throw snowballs at m—Ow!" I groan.

"Where are we going? We've been walking on the mountain for hours. My legs are about to melt," Davian complains.

"You can walk another ten hours, the rest of us can walk just ten meters more," Alassia says, looking at a cave at the far end.

"Ow!" Franz howls when I throw a snowball at him.

"Gotcha!" I say.

Franz scowls. Then, he grins. "You wanna play dirty? I can give you dirty!"

He throws a snowball at me. I throw one back. Then, we realise everyone has walked ahead, and we run to catch up with them.

In front of me, is a cave. Cobwebs, bats… It might also have a huge polar bear or something.

"Can I not make a house out of ice instead?" I ask.

Everyone gives me the angry-eyes.

"You could have said that earlier, so we wouldn't have walked so much," Davian whines.

"I'll get to work," I say. "First, I need ice!"

"Right over there." Kelly points to the right.

I summon the ice towards me. I turn the ice into eight separate villas. I also put names on it to show which one is whose.

"There you go, folks," I say.

Everyone bolts to their villa. Fenna *literally* does. I go inside mine.

It's just one storey, with one room, one bathroom, and nothing else. I also created a training course outside the houses, so we can train. I go into my room.

The bed looks really comfy. It's more like a bed made of ice with snow as the mattress. The look of the bed makes me want to drop in. I jump into the ice bed, and my legs start to relax. In a blink of an eye, I start snoring. I get a dream. Sadly, it is about the scarface.

He is standing in his room. He looks at his lieutenant, Drake. He grabs his jet-black estoc, a long slim sword.

"Guard the lair. I'm going hunting," he says to Drake.

Then, he dashes out of the room. He goes out of the lair. Then, he takes a Pegasus and rides it. The Pegasus looks strangely familiar. The same plain white skin. The same long wings. Oh no! Flake. Zephyr must be forcing Flake to follow my scent. Zephyr rides Flake on the same route we took. Precisely.

"Danica, wake up. Breakfast," Kelly says.

"Oh no! Flake!" I say as I wake up. "Uh, I mean… uh, yeah, coming."

Kelly rolls her eyes.

"Actually," I say, sitting on my bed, "we should go find Andy and Archie."

"Good idea." Her expression darkens.

"So, let's get going," I urge.

"First stop, Franz," Kelly says, rushing off.

"Wait, why Franz?" I run after her.

Kelly knocks at his villa's door but no reply.

I think I hear Kelly saying, "That sleepy head!"

She pushes open the door and stomps into the bedroom.

"Wake up, sleepy head!"

"Ahh! I can't see! Heeeeelp! He—" he says. Suddenly, he blinks out of sleep. "Ahh! When did you come?"

"We've been standing here for two minutes," Kelly complains.

"Knocking on your door for even longer," I add.

"And… why did you, uh, come to me, specifically? Am I late for some war meeting? Or to see you guys blow up Zephyr's face?" Franz asks.

"Are you on the same planet as us? Or are you still in your dream world? We *never* have war meetings. We've never had one. Plus, it wouldn't matter to Zephyr if he gets blown. He'll just revive," Kelly states.

"Anyways, back to the point," I say, desperately. Then I look at Kelly so she could go ahead and talk.

"Can we know where our brothers are?" she asks.

Franz takes a deep breath, trying to concentrate, and after a few seconds, says, "The guys are in a car factory. They look young, about eight or nine years old."

Kelly and I exchange happy looks that show, *Thank goodness they're okay!*

"Where are they?" I ask.

"In… Vinnesse. Florington. The factory is called *Phoenix Air — Car Factory*. They're employed. They make cars to earn. Do you know what I mea—" Franz says.

"Thanks. Bye! Tell everyone to go anywhere but here, and inform them that we're going on a rescue mission."

Franz looks confused, but nodds obediently. He senses the urgency in my voice. We rush out of Franz's villa.When we get outside, Kelly asks, "Why do they need to go somewhere other than here?"

"I had a dream just now. He has Flake. And, I don't want to involve the team in this risky mission. Now, come on," I reply."Ok. We should hurry then. Let's go by boat; I'll make the boat, and you get the water. Okay?" Kelly suggests.

I nod.

I gesture for some water to come towards me. From somewhere in the mountains, I finally get enough. While I am doing that, Kelly quickly draws a boat and swipes it out. The boat is a small rowboat. I step in followed by Kelly. Then, I make the water go under the boat, lifting it half a metre higher. I control the water to move forward, taking the boat with it.

"Ugh!" I say as the water goes forward but without us.

I try again. This time we are moving. The job I took is quite tiring because, after an hour, I feel almost dead.

Thankfully, a real ocean comes by. This means I can go for a relaxing swim. I take the boat into the ocean. I dive into the water and do nothing. I don't move a muscle. Like anyone, I start to float upwards. I stay in the water. After half an hour, I climb onto the boat and continue with the Captain's job.

Who knew a peaceful boat ride was unaffordable for us? I did. But still, I didn't predict it would be in the middle of the sea, and we would be surrounded by evil fishes!

Jet-black fish circle our boat in synchronisation. They show off their vampire-like teeth, naturally black. Every minute, one of the fish jumps out of the ocean and dives right onto us — almost — revealing their body. Unlike how they look in the ocean, the fish here are bigger than a blue whale.

Kelly says, "They are toxic whales. I remember that evil fish book I read once. The toxic whale has a flexible skeleton and can bend from any part of its body. Its pupils are also black. The body of the fish is coated with a fine layer of poison. One touch and we are dead."

The fish keep diving like dolphins. Then, as if *he* gave them the signal, they suddenly stop and start facing us like sharks. The whales scowl. They show off their banana-sized sword-sharp teeth. Just as they do that, *he* comes, my *lovely* old — very old — friend, Zephyr, with my loyal mate, Flake. The toxic whales float around the boat as Flake and Zephyr land.

"Where are you off to in the middle of the sea? You weren't with your friends, so I started to get worried," Zephyr asks.

"You found them?" I ask, perturbed.

"Ha! Found them? I captured them," he reveals. "If you're going to meet your brothers, by the way — I knew you'd be — take me along. I am guessing you know where they might be."

"Uh, get out of my ship. We've no idea where we're going," I command. "Leave Flake with me."

"As you wish, Madam!" He bows. With that, he dives out of the ship leaving Flake with me.

"Huh?" I ask Kelly.

"I've absolutely no idea what just happened," Kelly claims.

"Ahh! I do, Kelly! Ahh! Help!" I say as a toxic whale — who we had completely forgotten about — sticks its teeth in my t-shirt and starts pulling me into the water.

Kelly comes running to me. She grabs my legs and starts pulling me away from the whale. Great! Now, I am a tug-of-war rope. Kelly vs. Toxic whale.

Oh no! The toxic whale is on the verge of winning… Look at that! Kelly pulls me with enormous force, almost to the winning point. Now, the whale is pulling me toward its side. They both are going back and forth, and using equal strength. They are about to stretch this rope (me) long enough to tear it in two. The rope cannot take it anymore. Suddenly, there is a winner. Apparently, Kelly doesn't have as much stamina as the whale.

She tires off before the whale, letting it pull me into the sea as dinner for its family.

The whale pulls me deeper. Deeper. The sea gets duskier. Duskier. The coral reef is gleaming in the dimness. The other fish in the sea uncourageously do not dare to swim within the one-kilometre radius of the whale. If a fish came closer — which, I assure you, happens only in 0.00000000000001% of cases — the whale would either scowl or eat up the fish in one gulp, which terrified me. Half of my t-shirt is already in the whale's mouth.

I cross my fingers, hoping that Kelly didn't dive into the sea after me. Most importantly, her t-shirt hopefully is not in a whale's mouth right now, with the whale dragging her to whatever rendezvous the sea-creatures have planned.

Suddenly, we stop. The whale lets go of my t-shirt and stays close. A dozen other whales surround me. They look at me as if there were a note on my stomach saying: *Fresh meat for free! Come and get some!*

They look like they are getting ready for lunch — in my head, I imagine them with forks and knives, and myself on a huge plate — but they don't eat me. Yes, they stare at me for ages, but they don't eat me. Hopefully, they are taking pity on me and are willing to let me go. However, my luck isn't that great.

Out of the corner of my eye, I see another whale appear, followed by Kelly. Kelly's face is flushed. Her eyes closed. She looks like she is running out of air. Oh! She is running out of air.

I silently make a small bubble to cover her face similar to the one that I made on the island. I hope Kelly isn't… I can't say the word. It's too painful. D. E. A. D. I get the urge to go and check on Kelly, but I am clever enough — I am the queen of clever, actually — to know better than that. Those hungry mouths are going to come at me any minute now.

A whale on my right looks at me with its bloodshot eyes. I could clearly understand that this one will take the first bite of me. I try to think of an escape plan. I feel like hitting my head with a club until the lightbulb in my head finally works. When I start to get highly desperate, I decide to grab Kelly and swim away. But, these whales will probably catch up. If only I had a boost.

A boost! My birthday shoes! I check my feet to see if I am wearing them. Yes! They are crimson red, probably because I am so scared. I quickly get up and grab Kelly. The whales look confused about how I courageously got up as if they didn't exist. Ofcourse, they start coming after Kelly and me.

I activate the boost. I speed up to three times as fast as I normally am. Woefully, the whales are much faster. They are very close to catching up. If I go on like this, the whales will surely beat us again.

I remember another feature Franz had told me about the shoes. Perfect! I press a button on my shoes. The button lights up. Suddenly, smoke is all around. Don't ask how it is smoking underwater, I have no clue. The next second, Kelly and I are back aboard the boat.

I wouldn't really have cared much about the boat, but I do care about something valuable in the boat. Flake.

"Flake?" I call out, "Flake!"

Suddenly, I see a white figure flying in the sky, ready to land. Soon, I hug Flake with a comforting smile. An idea pops up in my head. Kelly and I could go to our brothers by the Pegasus instead of the boat. It is a faster option.

We climb onto Flake and soar through the sky for nearly an hour or so. We land in Florington, in front of the same car factory Franz had described to us.

We take a deep breath, cross our fingers, and step inside.

The factory is filled with machines, a machine for spray painting cars, a machine for drilling, a conveyer belt etc. Everyone seems so focused, I wonder if they ever get distracted.

Kelly and I walk further. At a distance, we see a door with a label saying: *Training sessions.*

We knock on the door and then open it. In here too, everyone seems focused. This room is filled with teenagers trying to learn how to make a car. There is a teacher going around the room making sure everyone is doing it right. We go forward and see a queue of a bunch of nine to eleven-year-old kids. They also have a teacher checking.

We go even further, across the queue, and see two red-haired boys working together on a small version of a car. There they are. My brothers. They have aged quite a lot since the last time I saw them, but they look the same.

They are quite indulged in their machinery. They don't notice us until I finally spoke.

"Andy, Archie?" I say.

They look up.

"You," Andy says, his fists clenched, "out!" He points at an exit.

What? This is nothing as I expected. I thought I would get a hug. But instead, I am being told to get out. What did I ever do to them?

"You come after two years! Whatever it is, we don't want to talk to you. You aren't allowed in here, so get out," Archie booms.

"Hey, wait," I say.

"No!"

"Can we at least tell you why we sailed all the way from Colzieu and even got attacked by whales on the way, just to see you guys?"

"Fine, only if you go out and never return once you're done." Andy agrees.

I start narrating everything that has happened since the last time we saw each other, including all the adventures we had. I hesitate before mentioning the Revenirs, but then I tell them about it anyway. I tell them about Zephyr and how he sent Dad to kill them. Then we share our journey to find them.

"Wow! I mean, everything except the 'dad trying to kill us' part. I am finding it difficult to come to terms with that part." Andy says.

"I am pretty surprised I am saying this, but can we join you?" Archie asks.

"That is pretty much our plan to save you."

"Are you allowed to go out of the factory without permission?" I ask.

"Not unless we wanna get extra work. It's tiring, the extra work," Archie says.

"But, if you go out and don't come back?"

"We will be known as escapees all around the city," Andy says.

"They will catch us in two seconds," Archie complains.

"How can you get expelled?" I ask.

"We can put the wrong wires together and create an explosion, right in front of our teacher's face," he says.

"Good idea. We'll wait in the far corner till then," Kelly says.

Before we could move a step, someone speaks behind us.

"Who are you?" The teacher questions.

"I am Georgia, and she is Clara," Kelly says quickly.

"Why are you here?"

"Are you questioning us?" Kelly asks. "For your information, we're junior inspectors, inspecting the work of these children. I suppose I will have to add your rudeness to my report."

"Oh! No, Madam. I was merely unaware. This is a surprise inspection, I suppose."

"Very well. You may continue," Kelly demands. "May I ask you to check the work of these two? It seems perfect."

"Sure!"

Kelly and I take a seat on the far corner, waiting for the explosion.

"Boom!"

Suddenly, the whole workshop is covered in ash. Andy and Archie, too, are covered. Even though the teacher is covered in black, he looks red. He inhales.

"Out of my workshop!" he bellows. "Make sure I do not see you again!"

"Yes, Sir!" Andy and Archie step out.

Normally, when a teacher shouts, one is sad. In this case, the twin brothers are giggling with excitement.

"We shall get going, Sir!" I say, and we exit the workshop.

When we are out, Kelly and I start snickering loudly.

I find Flake, and all four of us hop on. We soar through the sky, having no idea where we are going. Somehow, Flake could find the right direction and, we finally, reach.

Well, we don't reach them, but we land on the same snowy mountains. We walk a little to find them, but they are nowhere to be seen.

We walk a little more, and there they are. We run towards them.

"Hi, guys!" I greet them, a little too excitedly to fit the mood. "What happened? Why the sad faces?"

"He was our only hope," Alassia cries.

"What is going on?" Andy asks.

"I am gonna kill Zephyr the next time I see him!" Franz booms.

-13-

Kidnap

"What is up? Guys!" I impatiently scream.

"He… died," Davian dramatically cries.

"Who?" I ask.

"The guy who lived since the WB," Franz says.

"WB?" Archie asks.

"World Bomb!"

I was still trying to process the information.

"Ahh!" Franz screams.

"You mean Ed?" I ask, wide-eyed.

"Yes. Him," they yell.

In a few minutes, Kelly and I end up sobbing with them. That was the last thing we expected, Master Ed being killed by Zephyr. We shouldn't have taken his immortality from him.

"If he is dead, who can defeat Zephyr?" I ask.

"I've no idea," Fenna admits.

"I am guessing we've no chance of beating him. We should probably prepare for the end of the world," I say, dramatically.

"Don't say that. We shall succeed. Maybe not the way we expect to but who knows?" Kelly tries to boost our confidence.

"What in all of humanity is going on?" Archie questions.

"Oh!" I realise they were standing on the side awkwardly, staring at us sobbing.

I wipe my tears.

"Who are you?" Davian questions.

"What are you doing here?" Alassia asks.

"Hey, wait! You guys are Danica's brothers?" Franz suggests.

"They look nothing alike! You boys have brown eyes and red hair, but you girls have blue eyes and brown hair, and there are a hundred more differences. You guys look nothing alike," Alassia says.

"Yeah, yet they're my — very infuriating — brothers," I state.

"I can relate. My younger brother is the most annoying," Franz says, agreeing.

"Since you're this irritating, I can't imagine how much more annoying he'd be," I suggest.

"Hey! If you don't mind, I'd not like to be called *annoying* or *irritating*!" Franz protests.

"Is it wrong to simply say the truth?" I ask.

"Ugh!"

"Anyway, this is Archie." I point at Archie. "And, this is Andy." I point at Andy.

"Don't mind if I call you by the wrong names. You're exceedingly identical," Alassia states.

"I suggest you don't get us confused," Andy demands. "It's for your own good."

"I'll try."

"Who are you guys? Tell us!" Andy enquires.

Everyone introduces themselves.

I would like to take a moment of silence for what my friends are about to endure next, given that both my brothers are highly dramatic.

"I heard you guys have some lame powers. Show me how lame your powers are," Andy orders.

One by one, they all show their powers. When they all are done, he opens his mouth. "Are you guys planning to save the world with dumb powers like that?"

We all look at each other. "Well, uhh… sort of, I guess."

"There is nothing dumber than that," Andy says, in a discouraging tone. "How on earth can you think of being superheroes with powers like that? Show your powers again, if you don't impress me, I'll strangle you," he commands.

"So, you're our leader or something?" Alassia asks.

"You! Alassia girl, don't ask questions. Do you understand? Show me your powers first. Go! Quick! Now!" He orders.

Alassia turns into a butterfly, then a peacock, and then several other things.

"Lame! Go to the lame corner! Now!" He points to his right.

"Davian, I want to see your powers! Show me!" He demands.

Davian makes himself move in slow motion and then superspeed.

"Boring! Lame corner! Go!" He bellows. He continues this until everyone, and even Archie, is in the lame corner.

"Now, time to strangle all of you." Andy kicks, punches, and does karate on all of us. We try to follow the act and pretend to fall. Though in reality, he is terrible at karate.

No matter how lame, Andy does a good job providing us with a bit of distraction from Master Ed's death.

"Now, show me again. If it is horrible, you get more horrible karate!" My kiddish brother booms.

"Andy, how about we try planning the defeat?" I ask.

"No! You have to get those stupid stunts better," Andy roars.

"Okay, that's it." I go to him and take him with me to the houses we had made before.

"Where are the houses?" I ask.

"Zephyr," Alassia says.

"Oh. Then, where do we go?" Kelly asks.

"Maybe hop onto Flake," I suggest.

We all sit on the Pegasus.

"Where exactly are we going?" Kelly asks.

"Erm…"

"When will you tell us about the prophecy? You told us that you will reveal that soon," Archie asks.

"*You will be betrayed by a teammate.*
The one you love will be someone you truly hate.
A big battle will come by
Where many will die
Guardian is Morning Star's fate," I recite.

"Which teammate will you be betrayed by?" he asks.

"We were betrayed by a girl with mind power, Lezabel."

"Who do you hate but you truly loved?"

"Dad."

"Dad?" He asks.

"Yes. Dad. I do not want to explain." Sorrow cracks my heart into pieces.

"Has the battle already come by?"

"Nope. But, it is bound to come soon, I think." I say.

"What was the last part of the prophecy?" He asks.

"Guardian is Morning Star's fate. I've no idea what that means."

"Wait a second, I have a hint as to what that might mean," Kelly suggests.

Everyone's eyes go to her.

"Master Ed just died, right? Which means that we need a new guardian."

"Are you suggesting that whoever is Morning Star will be the new guardian?" Davian asks.

"Exactly," Kelly says.

"Who is Morning Star?" I ask.

"When shall we decide where to land?" Alassia asks

"Oh, right."

I try to think. Where could we land? We have done Auberfort, Colzieu, Vinnesse — Kelly and I have, at least.

"We haven't done Alenzon and Glazenia," I say.

"Let's go to Alenzon. I like Alenzon," says Andy.

"I wasn't suggesting Glazenia anyway," I mutter.

"Okay. Alenzon it is!" Kelly agrees.

"Where in Alenzon?" Alassia asks.

"Tarrabelle."

We fly for hours and hours. It is the most boring ride. Understanding the mood, Alassia starts singing songs, which is an insult to injury. Her singing, trust me, is like hearing a cat scratching the chalkboard.

"Danica, would you kindly ask your Pegasus how many more years will it take to reach?" Franz whines.

"If by years you mean minutes, it will take two years," Kelly says, pointing at the lit city only a few miles away.

I barely hear the last part because, by that time, I am fast asleep. This time, I get a dream.

I am about four years old, sitting on my mum's lap. Mum reads me a bedtime story. One of my favourites. Morning Star is its name. After reading the book, she shares a fact about me — a fact I don't remember.

"Danica, wake up! Danica!" They shake me and hit me until I wake up.

"Yeah, I am awake." I open my eyes.

"Took half an hour to wake you up!" Alassia complains.

"Let's check the city; it seems cool!" I say with my eyes widened.

The whole city is awake. Lights are hanging everywhere. In the centre of the city stands a vast stage. People are dancing and showing off their skills on it. Music is loud enough for people to hear across the city. This festival, as I recall, is the festival of Kalena. Kalena is when everyone in Alenzon shows off their talents. It is one of the most famous festivals celebrated across the globe. It must be 10th July, today.

We go to some stalls: The Dance Devil, Rubik's Cube Rockstars, and Knitting Kompetitors.

After the stalls come the sports stadiums. Sports like football, basketball, roller skating, ice skating, and skateboarding are taking place there.

The sports stadiums lead to the grandest location of them all.

The spotlights dance, shining their light on the vast wooden stage. On the top of the stage, is a huge banner: *Alenzon's Got Talent*. The crowd is cheering and clapping their hands in anticipation. In front of the stage, is a judges' table occupied by three judges.

At the table, there sits a woman with a dull wrinkled face and brown eyes. Her brown hair, with highlights, curl into a bun on her head. She is wearing ink black clothes.

The second judge is a man who seems to be twinning with that woman. But, instead of a bun, his hair is spiked. His face, rather than dull, has the widest smile ever seen before. His eyes are glowing. He sits back, enjoying the show.

The third judge is a woman with grey eyes, also glowing. Her brunette hair is in a short pigtail. She seems to be on the verge of clapping but resisting so she doesn't disrupt the show.

On the vast stage, stands, the one and only, Clara Hughes. Clara is the most famous dancer in the world. Well, second-most. She has brown wavy hair with highlights, blue eyes, and pale skin. Her choice of clothes is splendid; it perfectly fits my taste. Her black leggings have a strip of pink on both legs. Her top is the most magnificent. It is also black, but it has pink fur on it. She looks marvellous.

I quickly take a seat to watch the show. Everyone else also sits. We start watching.

Clara somersaults in the air and does a few ballet twists. She performs a smooth dance. After her dance, she comes to the middle of the stage and checks the reactions of the judges. Obviously, she isn't very satisfied with the expression on the first judge's face.

"That. Was. Awesome!" The other two judges say.

"That was awful!" The first judge says in a snappy voice.

"Stop being such a bitter judge, Linda!" The male judge says. His voice is a pure BBE British accent.

"Stop being so light on the performers, Carl!" Linda says.

"Ignore Linda's unjust judgment. Now, may we see the next performer?" The third judge says.

"My judgement is way squarer than yours, Amy," Linda argues.

"Now, now, may we stop bickering and listen to this performer?" Carl suggests.

Sia Day enters. The crowd stands up and cheers. Sia opens her mouth and sings infinite times better than Alassia. She ends with her hand holding the mic in the air, like cool rappers at the end of a song.

After the song, comes gymnastics.

She performs a floor routine full of somersaults. Then, she does a few cool tricks on the bars. After a few flips and cartwheels, she does handstands on the balance beams.

We watch a few more shows until we end up snoring on the seats.

When I wake up, the sun is shining bright. No one is in the audience seats but me, my dear friends and siblings.

"Guys, wake up!" I shake everyone.

After everyone is up and back to their senses, I ask, "Where are we going to live? Should we rent a house?"

"Probably," Fenna says lazily. "Wait, what? Are you crazy? We don't have the money to rent a house."

"Hahaha, got you awake!"

"So, to answer your question, we can build a shelter," Kelly says.

"Very helpful!" I roll my eyes.

"How about we go for a walk," Davian says.

As we walk, we talk about how awesome the previous day's show was. The last time we had that much fun was during Kelly's and my birthday party. After Master Ed's death, the only emotions we felt were intense sorrow and hate. The show was a great way to lift our moods and a great distraction from everything else going on.

"I feel pretty filthy. Let's take a bath!" I suggest.

"Let's go there!" Fenna points at the spa.

"Uhh… there are boys who don't like spas," Franz gives a reminder.

"Let's split up, then. You boys go your separate ways, and we girls go our separate ways," Alassia says.

"Cool. We will meet near that fountain at sunset," Azteque says.

After the boys leave, we start moving towards the spa.

We enter the spa to find a luxurious hallway with a gold and marble theme. We go to the counter for check-in. Kelly, going against everything she stands for, draws us three 500 bucks notes. Once we have paid, a lady comes in and leads us to a room. We lie on the spa beds and allow the ladies to do everything for us. There is a lady putting on a face mask on me and another lady doing my nails, while my legs are dipped in a bucket of water. Once the face mask is put on and cucumbers cover my eyes, I just lie there with a sense of freshness.

After an hour, we come out of the spa feeling rejuvenated and brand new.

"Ahh!" I say. "I've got to admit, that was great, except for these flowers in my hair." I pull out the flowers gently, trying not to dismantle my hairstyle. Since when have I started caring about my hair?

"Now, let's have a nice and calm walk?" Fenna suggests.

After walking and talking for about two hours, it starts to get dark, and we decide to go to the fountain and wait for the boys.

After twenty minutes of searching for the fountain, I ask, "Wait a second, doesn't this house look like the same one we passed before?"

"Don't tell me we've been going in circles this whole time," Alassia whines.

"So, I guess we're lost," Kelly says.

A girl, the only person in the street, walks by. I wonder if all the people in this place sleep early.

"Excuse me? Hello!" I call out. We go running after her.

"Where can we find the fountain?" Fenna asks.

"There are millions of fountains here, girl!" I say and punch Fenna on her arm.

"Where can I find the spa?" She rephrases the question.

"Take the third left, and then the second right. From there, if you keep going straight, you will end up at the fountain," she directs. Her black hood covers her face. She doesn't look up either. Her voice is very soft and shy.

"Ha! She said fountain. That means she knows which fountain. I was correct," Fenna says, lifting an eyebrow.

"How do you do that?" I ask.

"How do I do what?"

"That lifting the eyebrow thingy!"

"You can't do it? It is easy. You command only one eyebrow to raise," she says, unhelpfully.

"That totally seems easy!" I taunt.

"Told you!"

"I was being sarcastic!"

"Come on, guys," Alassia calls us.

We start walking. The route the girl has given us seems different from the way we came through earlier. I am pretty sure we didn't pass these houses and shops.

"Fenna, why do you keep punching me?" I ask.

No reply. I turn around. No one.

I hear a muffled noise.

"Huh? Fenna?"

I turn to my front again. No one.

"Guys?" My voice echoes in the night. The atmosphere resembles the start of a horror book.

"Hello?" I whimper.

Pull it together, Danica.

"This is not a joke!" I yell.

Someone punches me on my back. I turn around. A guy in black sprays something on me. I collapse.

When I wake up, I am tied to a pole in an empty warehouse. The thing tying me to the pole is not a rope; it is not a chain either. It seems more like a rope made of metal — if that is possible. How do I break this thing? I can control water, but not metal!

Whoever tied me with this metal rope must be incredibly strong to be able to bend metal. Alhough, I bet there isn't anyone strong enough to bend metal as heavy as this.

Wait a minute… potion. That's it! That kidnapper must have been working for Zephyr. The girl who led us here must have been Lezabel. No wonder she hid her face!

Ok, now I really need to get myself free from this metal rope-thing. It is squishing me.

I simply need to figure out a way to cut this metal. If only I had water. There doesn't seem to be a single drop of water around. Wait a second, am I underground? There has to be water in the sewer next to this place.

I focus on the water in the sewer. It is hard to control the water as my hands are stuck in the metallic rope. I slowly burst the sewers and direct the water to come to me.

-14-

Memories and Reunion

"Hey! Don't you even try to think of anything clever," someone says coming towards me.

I quickly put the water back in the sewer and seal it with ice. The person is in black; only his eyes can be seen. He is probably the same guy who sprayed perfume at me.

"Don't try to escape. I need to get you to Zephyr as soon as possible," he warns.

"Where are my friends?" I try to shout, but with the rope choking me, the words are unclear.

"They're somewhere safe, don't worry. It is just you who we need. Your friends will probably be separated or killed. Well, that is nothing for you to worry about." His cold voice echoes.

"Why do you need me? I am not different from the others."

"Oh, well, you aren't. You will be, though!" He comes closer by the second.

"How?"

"*Guardian is Morning Star's fate.* Morning star. Does it remind you of anything?" he asks.

"It reminds me of the book that Mum used to… Wait, how do you know about the prophecy?" I question.

"Have you heard of the death of your stupid Master Ed? You know that Ed was the one who last had the book of prophecies, correct? Maybe Zephyr just stole it. I mean, why not," he reveals.

He what! So, the book of prophecies is currently in the wrong hands. Damn!

"Anyways, I've got to wait outside to check if the Pegasus to export you is here yet. Try not to get in trouble. Trust me, you would rather prefer to suffer without getting in trouble than suffer after getting in trouble." He walks out.

Now, I have a different plan. I am gonna wait.

The next day, the man comes again. He takes a sharp knife and cuts the part attaching the metallic rope to the pole. But, the rope continues to choke me. He grips my arm, real tight, and pulls me to the Pegasus. This is going perfectly, as I have planned, except for the part where the rope is still around me. Now, I wait for us to fly.

As we soar through the sky, the man keeps an eye on me. He doesn't look at anything but me. I try to find the right time.

The man suddenly looks away to see where we are. My mind suddenly shouts, *"Now!"*

I immediately seize the opportunity and jump. As soon as the man realises the escape I just made, he dives after me. Obviously, since I dived before him, I was lower than him. However, I guess he took a backpack with him, making him heavier. He, eventually, catches up to me.

He holds on to my leg. I take water from the clouds, and use it to make his hand slip. It does slip. He continues falling faster than me. While he is falling, I use the water from another cloud to make a platform for me to stand on, so I don't fall flat on the ground. I use the platform like a hoverboard.

Luckily, my idea was good, and I land on the board. I'm not even slightly injured. I have no idea where I am. I can't see the man either. I am still separated from my friends. Hopefully, they are safe and one of them finds me.

I realise I am on the top of a building. I jump down. Normally, if Mom were here, she would be like, *"Why did you just jump off a building?"* My heart gives a slight sob at the mention of the word 'Mom'. Get over it, Danica!

I look around. Why does this place seem so familiar? I keep walking. As I walk, the realisation slowly comes to me. Is this… No, it can't be! Then, I pass the one thing I didn't want to see, ever again!

The door tried to shoo me away. The whole house tried to shoo me away. I am not interested in going back there. It will remind me of sad things. It will remind me of my family. It will remind me of Mom.

My anger suddenly returns. My rage persuades me to punch and kick this hideous house. My harsh breath indicates my fury.

I fall to the ground and hug my knees, crying, as I did two years ago in the hut, after gaining knowledge of Mum's death.

Before I even notice, I am fast asleep. This time, I get a dream of the insides of my house. Does Alice want to give me a nightmare?

It feels like a tour of the house. I hear footsteps. First, I see the living room. The dining room comes next. Then comes the kitchen. I see the rooms upstairs. I am going downstairs again. The dream shows me the door. A hand holds the doorknob. Slowly, it opens the door.

I wake up as the door I am leaning on opens. Wait a second! Was my dream showing me that someone is in my house and just opened the door? I turn around to see who opened the door.

"Kelly?" I ask.

"Danica?" she asks.

We hug each other.

"You're safe!" We say together.

"How are you here?" I wonder.

"A guy kidnapped us and separated us. I've been trying to find everyone. I found this place as I walked," she tells.

"A guy kidnapped me and tied me to a pole with this metallic rope. He was going to export me to Zephyr, but I escaped mid-air."

"Why you?"

"He said something about the statement in the prophecy. *Guardian is Morning Star's fate.* He asked me if it reminds me of anything at all."

"Speaking of the prophecy, I think I've figured it out. I think you're meant to be the next guardian. I've no idea how you will become the guardian, but being the guardian is in your fate," Kelly says.

"Wait, what?" I ask.

"Remember that Morning Star book, the one Mum used to read to us?" she asks. "When Mum read it to us, she used to tell a fact about Morning star. It is the meaning of your name. Danica."

"Now I remember!"

"Now, we need to find everyone and defeat Zephyr. Where can everyone else possibly be?" Kelly brings the topic back up.

"I am guessing, scattered around the globe?"

"How do we reunite?" she asks.

"How about we check every inch of the world? Let's start over there!" I insist.

"Ugh!" Kelly rolls her eyes.

"Man, I hate Zephyr so much!" I groan.

I keep trying to think of an idea and save the day, but my light bulb won't light. Kelly does the same, but her light bulb won't light either.

"How about we go away from this house, first?" I insist.

"Agreed."

We walk away. We go to the park and sit on the swings. I try not to think about anything unhappy. I just swing, on and on. I also go onto the big circular swings that have a weblike shape on the inside. I lie there, enjoying the soothing wind.

The kids play with joy. Their laughter reminds me of those times when my friends and I would play together. I remember the last time we were together; we played Coltivyx. After that, we never saw each other. After that, everything changed. Stop it, Danica. No thinking about anything negative.

Suddenly, I hear a familiar voice. Is it just in my head? Or is she here? I sit up to see if it isher. The sight makes my day. There she is, my best friend, entering the park.

As quick as light, I run to her. As I run, tears of joy run down my face. For the first time in years, euphoric tears run down my face. She freezes in shock the second she sees me.

"Danica," Trucia asks, "is that really you?"

"Yes!"

"I can't believe it! After all these years," she says, gleefully. "Why did you never come back again?" she asks.

"I shifted," I lie.

"Without telling us?"

"I didn't get the chance to."

"How are you here, then?" she asks.

"I wanted to see you, so I asked my dad to drop me off," I continue lying.

"Where are your parents?"

"Back at my house." I lie The word 'parents' strikes me. I hold back a sob.

"How about we play something for a bit, while I am still here?" I suggest. Meanwhile, I direct the water from her wet body to go back to where it came from, so that she is dry again.

"I've half an hour more. Let's make the most of this time," she states.

"Running race? Two rounds of the track?" I challenge.

"I am beating you!"

We go on the starting line.

When we are ready, Trucia shouts, "On your marks! Get set! Go!"

I run as fast as possible. I remember the tips for running. Long strides. Your arms should go from your hip to your lips. Your head is the heaviest part of your body. Lean forward when running so that your head drags you forward. These tips can increase my speed by seconds.

I realise this race isn't fair because I have cool superpowers, have been in wildly dangerous situations, and been training for two years. It seems to me, this competition is one-sided.

I realise Trucia is a few hundred miles behind me. I decide to slow down, just so Trucia can try to catch up. I am done with two rounds of the track by the time Trucia is done with her first lap.

"I beat you! Ha!" I brag.

"Ugh!"

"That was fun," I exclaim.

"What part? The part when you won? Or the part when you bragged about winning? Or the part when you saw the look of defeat on my face?" she asks.

"Well, all of the parts."

"Let's see if you can beat me in a workout race," she challenges.

"You already know the chances of you winning."

"Obviously! I've cent per cent chances of winning."

"Right, we will see. We do 100 push-ups, 50 burpees, 150 jumping jacks, and 50 sit-ups. The first one to do all that, stand up, and clap their hands three times, wins," I say.

"Ready?" she asks.

I nod.

"Set. Go!" she yells.

I complete 100 push-ups in one minute, followed by a ten-second break. I am not yet tired. Next, I do fifty burpees and take another ten-second break. Now, my breathing is fast. I continue with 150 jumping jacks, then pause for another ten seconds. This time, my breathing is even faster. Finally, I perform fifty sit-ups. As quick as a flash, I get up and clap my hands three times. By the end, I am breathless.

When I am back in form to stand up, I realise that Trucia wasn't too behind me. Only thirty seconds.

"Considering the fact that you were only thirty seconds slower than me, good job," I say, generously.

"In the running race, you brag. In the workout race, you do a humble brag," she states.

"I'd like a thank you!"

Suddenly, Franz and Azteque pop out of nowhere.

"Hey there, having fun?" Franz asks.

"We were worried," Azteque says.

"What the hell!" Trucia screams, her voice filled with horror. We all just ignore her.

"What are you doing here!" I yell.

"Franz couldn't see you anywhere in Alenzon," Azteque says.

"This is not the time!"

"Aw, sweetheart, I apologise for disturbing your quality time with your friend while a war is approaching." Franz's voice was laced in sarcasm with every word he spoke.

"War?" Trucia's eyes widened.

"We got worried that you were taken by Zephyr or something!" Azteque said, ignoring Trucia.

"What is going on?" Trucia asks. "Who are you guys? How did you appear out of nowhere?"

"Uhh…" Azteque widens his eyes. "Got to go! Come on, Dan."

He grabs both of us and teleports us to Alenzon again, where I find everyone waiting for us.

"What on earth is wrong with you?" I boom.

"How am I supposed to know you're catching up with an old friend today out of all times," Franz says.

"Don't you have super eyes?" I ask.

"We really don't have time for this!" Azteque cuts in.

"My friend is probably wondering what just happened, and she is probably thinking that I just ditched her. Again. All because of you!"

"Look, I'm sorry. I get it, trust me. I miss my old life more than anything," Franz says, with a lot more loss and longing than he seemed to be letting on. He swallows.

Azteque continues for him, "But we really need you to stay focused for now. Only until all of this is over. We cannot afford to be distracted. Please, understand."

I nod, understanding that sacrificing my old life may not be easy, but I'll always have this group who can understand what that feels like. Maybe the reunion with Trucia was good for closure.

-15-

No Pain No Gain

"So, where do we go? Where do we take shelter?" Davian asks.

"Let's... Uhh... go... umm... to... I don't know," I say blankly.

"I can get money out of my drawing. We can use the money to get a house," Kelly insists.

"What?" I ask. This is not Kelly. Did she just agree to cheat, again?

"I was about to ask if Kelly could draw a house itself," Franz suggests.

"Good idea!" Kelly starts to sketch.

After about five minutes, when she is done drawing, she asks, "Give me a good place to set up the house."

"Over there!" I point at a row of houses nearby.

She places the house exactly where I pointed.

"Voila!"

I rush into the house. The bed in my room is so relaxing and soft. The second I lay on it, I fall asleep. It is a dreamless sleep, thankfully.

When I wake up, I feel fresher. I lie on the bed lazily for half an hour. When I finally get off the bed, Kelly knocks.

"Danica, wake up. Come downstairs to the living room," she calls out from the other side of the door.

"Okay," I reply.

I quickly take a shower and go downstairs.

"There you are," Kelly says. "We were just gonna go underground and train."

"Underground?" I ask.

"Oh, yeah. I made an underground training area to do the stuff we don't want others to know about."

Kelly drags me outside my room, still half asleep, and asks me to push the sofa aside. She pulls out a tile from the floor to reveal a tunnel going downwards. Kelly jumps in first. I follow. Everyone else comes behind me. Alassia pushes the sofa back to how it was. She turns into a bird and goes under the sofa and into the tunnel. As she is falling, she turns into a human.

Kelly has placed a huge pillow right where we are supposed to fall, so that we experience a soft-landing.

Once everyone has landed on the pillow, we get off and go towards the training area. The place is gigantic; I am pretty surprised Kelly made this. There are three sections. One is a training area for the Revenirs. In that area, there are four courses and a lot of empty space — clearly, it is still not done. The other two sections has nothing at all.

"Wow!" I exclaim.

"Guys, since those two sections still need to be made, we will need to multitask. Andy and Archie, since you guys have already seen our powers, you can start making your training obstacles there." Kelly points towards one of the empty sections.

Andy and Archie get to work.

"The rest, make your course. When you're done making your course, you can start practising on them. Now go! We're starting with me," Kelly instructs.

I try making a plan to create my own course. I can add balls and arrows shooting at me, walls moving up and down, archery, and much more.

I dive right into making all these things. First, I make a track. The track leads to lava-hot water, and the only way to cross the lava-hot water, without touching it, is by the wall on its side. I need to climb the wall till I reach the place where the track starts again.

After wall climbing, it's time for archery. A large bucket filled with ice rocks is suspended above. I have to hit the target perfectly in the middle while running on the treadmill to stop the rocks from falling on me. Kelly designed this setup for me. The treadmill serves two purposes: to ensure I don't skip archery practice and to make it more challenging.

Next comes the balls. I need to run across the track while the balls keep shooting from ahead.

Once I cross the balls, I need to go for the long jump. There is lava-hot water, again. This time, I need to jump across the water, instead of climbing a wall.

After that, comes the final challenge: the high jump. There are five walls. The first wall is my height. The second is double the height of the first. The third is double the second and so on. I need to jump onto the first wall. From there onto the second, third, and so on.

When I am done making the course, I see all around me. There is so much progress. Azteque and Alassia are done making their courses. Fenna, Franz, and Davian are still making theirs. Archie and Andy are making theirs in the other section. Kelly is drawing training bots and a fighting ring for the third section.

Since I am done creating my obstacles, I try out my course. I go onto the track and walk towards the hot water. I try to climb the wall. Obviously, I am allowed to use my powers for climbing the wall. I summon water and turn them into two knives. I poke them into the wall and pull them out to move sideways. It takes me ages to reach the other end. I jump off, without the knives, and move on.

I take the bow and arrow, and get ready to hit. I hesitate. Taking a deep breath, I release. The arrow shoots speedily toward the board. A feeling of dizziness crosses me. At the back of my head, I think, *What if it doesn't hit?* I realise what a bad archer I am. The rocks come raging onto me and bruise me as hard as they can. I fall on my stomach, which is disastrous, as I am on a treadmill. The treadmill takes me to the end of it. Ouch! After that, I urge myself to stand. After a lot of trying, I get up on my feet. I go for the balls now.

Apparently, I am bruised. This means I can't run, duck, or do anything as easily. As the balls come shooting at me, I get hit by three of them. The first ball knocks me onto the floor. The second ball pushes me backwards. The third ball pushes me onto the treadmill again. This time, luckily, I manage not to get hurt by the treadmill. I am forced to redo this level, aren't I? Ugh!

I take an arrow and aim. I hesitate again. I take a deeper breath this time. I release. Thankfully, it hits. I pass the challenge without getting bruised. Thank God!

I go for the balls, again. I am still bruised, so I jog on the spot. After a few deep breaths, I feel I am ready, and make the run for it. A ball shoots towards me. I sidestep and dodge. Another ball comes my way; I slide under it. I evade every ball that flies at me. Victoriously, I reach the end.

Next – the long jump. I put my feet on the edge. My knees bend, and I swing my arms. I take a deep breath. When I am ready, I launch. I land on one foot, on the track. The other foot is about to go into the water. Before I lose balance, I put my second foot on the track. I move forward, towards the last obstacle.

I jump onto the first wall successfully, then the second, the third and the fourth. When I successfully reach the fourth wall,

I get myself ready. I have never attempted a jump as high as this. Once ready, I launch. At first, I think I might make it, but then, I realise I am not high enough. I am probably about to fall from 80 feet high — I have done the math. Unbelievably, I end up on top of the fifth wall. Here's how: I simultaneously summon water and turn them into two knives. I use the knives to grab onto the wall. I climb up the same way I climbed on the other wall. After I am on the wall, I jump down, from 80 feet. I give myself a pat on the back for successfully completing the course.

"Kelly, I've completed my course, and I am done patting myself on the back for successfully completing it. Now, what do I do?" I ask.

"You can probably try figuring out how you will be the guardian. Also, I'd like you to tell everyone else about your being the guardian. Maybe today, after dinner," she suggests.

I go up to my room. Well, going up the tunnel is way easier than I thought. Someone must have installed rocks to be used for climbing up to the living room. They weren't there before. I am guessing Alassia shapeshifted into a flying animal and installed them while I was making my course.

When I reach the top and push the tile, I realise that I am not thin enough to squish under the sofa. I summon water and turn it into a stick. I use the stick to push the sofa aside. After I go out, I close the entry and push the sofa back where it was.

In my room, I try figuring out how I will become a guardian. *A guardian needs to have all the powers, which means I need to have all the powers. How will I get them ? If I touch someone else's mole, it won't really give me the powers because I am not the guardian yet. What if someone else touches my mole? What will happen? Will I get their power? I can try it tonight!*

Suddenly, the bell rings. Rapidly, I go downstairs. I push the sofa and open the tile. I dive headfirst into the tunnel, landing on my hands. I swiftly stand up.

"Guys, the doorbell! Come up," I call.

Simultaneously, we climb up the tunnel, close the tile, and push the sofa. I go ahead to open the door.

Uh-oh!

"Hello, friends!" Zephyr greets.

"Hello!" Franz says, and I punch his shoulder. "Err… I mean… What are you doing here?"

"I merely came to say hi, and, give you a hint about the war coming up next week," he says.

"Next week?" Alassia asks. "Why next week?"

"My army is not prepared. We have to get things ready," he tells.

"Where is the war going to be?" I ask.

"I will give you a hint: awful, ugly, bad, exhausting, ruthless, fearless, obnoxious, rude, tiger," he answers. "Anyways, I better get going. Bye!" He leaves.

We just stand staring at the door as it closes behind him. That was the weirdest visit ever – the weirdest conversation with Zephyr. What on earth was that all about? "What the…" I say, stunned.

"Gosh, that was weird. Crazy weird." Franz agrees.

"We've only one week! Andy and Archie are nothing close to being prepared," Kelly complains.

"Let's get them prepared," Alassia suggests.

"How about we relax today, and start their training tomorrow?" I suggest.

I go upstairs for something relaxing. I switch the tap on for the bath. I first lie on my bed, waiting for the tub to be filled with water. After five minutes, I go and check the tub. The water is filled to the top. I put a lavender bath bomb. I switch on the royal blue LED lights that Kelly had kindly installed and switch off the washroom lights. Excited, I jump into the bath. Ahh!

The lavender fragrance refines my nostrils. Like clouds in the sky, the cotton white bubbles float in the water. The warm water soothes my skin. Glowing in the dark, the LED lights refresh my mind, erasing all the stress I have. The peaceful silence clears my mind. The atmosphere is tranquil enough for me to fall asleep. Slowly, I close my eyes. Even after my eyes being shut, I don't fall asleep, which is amusing. I stay in the bath for hours until I finally realise it's about to be dinner time. I let the water clear out. I wash out all the soap on me. I dry myself and dress up.

When I step out of the washroom, my body feels lighter, as if I just lost 10 kg. I lie on the bed. I grab a gaming console and start the HTV. I put on a horse-riding game.

As I play the game, Kelly comes in.

"Hello! Wanna play?" I ask.

"Sure!" She grabs the second console and jumps onto the bed. After almost an hour of extreme competitive gaming, Kelly wins.

"Haa! I beat you, loser! Haha!" Kelly taunts.

After losing, I decid it is better that I don't play with Kelly anymore. I leave the console and go downstairs.

"Danica, would you mind chopping the vegetables for pizza? Kelly, please get the pizza-sauce ready," Alassia orders.

I go on and help in the kitchen.

When dinner is ready, we all go into the stone dining room to eat. As I take a bite off my delicious pizza — its cheese stretching like elastic — I chat with my friends. Rather than talking about the battle coming up in a week, we talk about other things. Random things. From hobbies, we go all the way to trees.

After dinner, everyone gathers in the living room, on the sofas. When everyone is focused and ready to listen, I open my mouth.

"Remember the prophecy: *Guardian is Morning Star's fate*? My mom used to read me a book called Morning Star. She told me that my name means Morning Star. Which means, *Guardian is Danica's fate,*" I say.

"You're supposed to be the guardian?" Franz asks.

I nod.

"How exactly will you be the guardian?" Alassia asks.

"I will need to take all your powers."

"Will you touch my mole to take my powers?" Kelly asks.

"No, because I am not the guardian yet. I think you need to touch my mole to give me your powers," I suggest.

"Won't it be dangerous for us to fight without powers against a guy who could literally kill us in one strike?" Fenna asks.

"Yeah, it would."

"Why should Danica be the guardian? It should be me," Franz says. "And, what if I don't want to give my powers?"

"Franz!" Alassia groans.

"Yeah, fine," he cries.

"Let's go to bed, tomorrow we need to train. We all need a good night's sleep," Kelly says.

I go upstairs and lie on my bed for about an hour until I finally pass out.

The next day, when I wake up, I drink some milk and go straight into training.

Stronger! Stronger! Stronger! I yell in my head as I punch the bag. My punches are wicked strong, but if I could make them stronger, they could push someone to Mars.

In the meantime, Kelly is doing her workout. She does a few jumping jacks, push-ups, sit-ups, burpees, and more.

We are doing a rotation. There are different training things to do, for example, climbing — the one Fenna is doing right now. This involves climbing things like walls, rocks, trees, and ropes.

After half an hour, we rotate. I do the climbing. First, I climb the wall using the same ice-knife technique. After that, I climb the rope. To be honest, it is not very hard to climb a 20-foot-tall rope. Way easier than rope climbing is fake tree climbing. The only reason why it is easy is that I have done it quite a lot. But it reminds me of climbing a real tree, which in turn reminds me of the time I fell down a tree and got bitten — almost eaten — by a tiger. I decide to simply get it over with and move on to rock climbing — my personal favourite. Normally, by rock climbing, you would think of a wall with fake rocks screwed to it. Here, rock climbing is done on a wall with real rocks — it gives the feel of climbing a real mountain.

We continue the rotation until everyone is done with everything. We take some rest for five minutes and start training again. I complete my course with similar results as last time. The only difference is that I dodge all the balls on my first try, and land on the fifth wall perfectly in the high jump, without having to summon ice knives.

We go upstairs and have a quick lunch. When we are done eating, we go out for a walk to digest our food. Exercising after eating is harmful. Plus, we all need rest.

We walk around the city. It is a nice weather today. It is warm with a cool wind. After an hour, we come back in and go into the hideout.

We do wrestling. I choose Kelly to fight against me. Kelly and I go to the ring.

We eye each other. When I am ready, I strike water at her. She dodges. She shoots her ninja stars at me. I dodge. The water turns into a fist as I turn my hand into one. I imitate a punch, the water literally punching Kelly. The force does push Kelly down. She lands on her back. Before she can get back up, I strike her a few hundred times. She keeps attempting to get up, but I push her back down. I keep continuing like that until Kelly gives up. I give her a hand.

She gets up and says, "Good game!"

"It was sort of one-sided," I say.

Before I know it, it is dinnertime. We have a long dinner. I eat till my stomach is about to explode. The last time I overate was during the party we had back in Glazenia before all of this happened. That was three years ago! We relax on the sofa a little bit.

"While we're sitting, let's figure out what Zephyr meant by: awful, ugly, bad, exhausting, ruthless, fearless, obnoxious, rude, tiger. How can a list of adjectives describing a tiger have anything to do with where the war is starting?" Kelly wonders.

"What if he has just given random words to keep our minds busy, but it is actually useless?" I insist.

"I don't think so," Fenna says.

"I feel he is talking about the tiger. Where do we find tigers?" Kelly asks.

"Colzieu," I say.

"Yes, I think the adjectives might be to keep us thinking," Azteque says.

"I think it is in Glazenia. Glazenia is home to the fastest tiger ever. It has a world record," Franz suggests.

"It could mean Glazenia or Colzieu! How do we pick one?" I ask.

"It could also mean Vinnesse. There is a machine tiger invented in Vinnesse that is awful, ugly, bad, exhausting, ruthless, fearless, obnoxious, and rude," Davian insists.

"Glazenia, Colzieu, and Vinnesse! What is left?" I say.

"Alenzon and Auberfort!" Fenna says.

"Ugh!" I say.

"It could be Alenzon!" Azteque suggests.

"How?" I ask.

"There is a tiger species called Alenzon!" he says.

"So, now we've simply cancelled out Auberfort," Kelly says.

"Out of Alenzon, Vinnesse, Colzieu, and Glazenia, which should we cancel?" I ask.

"I think we should cancel Glazenia. Zephyr did not say anything about the tiger being fast, but the world record is about the fastest tiger," Alassia suggests.

"Now, we've Alenzon, Vinnesse, and Colzieu," I say, putting a strike against Glazenia on my paper.

"Cancel Vinnesse. I remember that the machine tiger was genial and generous, not obnoxious," Davian says.

"Now, we've Alenzon and Colzieu," I say.

"I just remembered that the tiger was named after Alenzon in a fictional book," Davian realises.

"I guess the war is in Colzieu," I exclaim.

Figuring that out was sort of hard. Ahem. It was hard.

For the next few days, we plan how we will attack. We create a Plan B, even Plan C. We decide exactly how I will take everyone's powers but still make it as safe as possible for them. We decide that we will leave two days before the war, on 18th July, which is in four days. It will take us only one day to reach, but in case something goes wrong, we don't want to arrive late.

-16-

Trip to war

According to the plan, we are meant to start packing everything for tomorrow. Tomorrow's ride is going to be long. We pack the plan layouts, food for the trip, and everything else we will need. When we are done packing, we get a good night's sleep, as we will need energy for tomorrow.

In the morning, when everyone is awake, we eat our breakfast. When it is about 10 a.m., we use the flying car that Andy and Archie had made. The seven Revenirs, Archie, and Andy enter the car. All our stuff is in the trunk of our car.

Guess who the pilot is? Andy and Archie! I still can't believe we let them do the driving. They bugged us during the whole two-hour drive and used their pilot microphone to send boring and dumb messages. Why did we let them add that microphone? Oh right, because they blackmailed us.

"Everyone, who likes songs, listen up. Well, lucky for you, we're professional singers," Archie exclaims on the mic.

With the most high-pitched voice, they sing, "La-la-la-la-la-laa! De-de-de-de-dee! Ho-ho-ho-ho-hoo!"

They crack my ears. They are even worse at singing than Alassia. Every five minutes, they are on the speaker coming up with a new ear-piercing 'song' — how can anyone consider it a song? Their tunes almost shattered the glass of the car.

The most annoying thing about my brothers is that they won't let me get any rest. My muscles are tired. My brain is dizzy. My eyes need rest. Still, they won't let me sleep.

Finally, I fall asleep.

I was hoping to wake up when we reach. Like always, I don't get what I want. I end up waking up when we crash. At least, I think, we were about to crash, judging by the way Andy screamed. Boy, I hate it when he fake-screams. We, fortunately, don't crash. Whereas, I, unfortunately, don't get sleep anymore.

After what seemed like ages, we reach. I am not, and will never be, too happy about reaching because arriving at Colzieu means that we are nearer to the war. As every passing second slips by, we are coming closer to it. It is like approaching your long-lost friend's door in a hallway — the door being the battle. If only I can know what happens at the end of the war, to decide if I want to step into this. I can always ask Davian to check the future for me, but even I know that knowing the future can be dangerous.

We step out of the car.

"Now what? The war is the day after tomorrow! What are we meant to do until then?" Kelly asks.

"I don't know. Maybe we could wait," Fenna suggests.

The sun looks like a gold pearl in the sky, ready to drop. After a few hours, the pearl finally drops and calls up its silver sister. The dark sky indicates that it's bedtime.

"Where should we settle for the night?" I ask.

"Maybe in our cars," Alassia suggests.

"Good idea, I am not in the mood for drawing," Kelly agrees.

"Seriously, is that even possible?" I ask.

"I am guessing, yeah. I myself did not know I can feel that way."

We all laugh.

I get into the car and lie on the seat. Luckily, there is enough room for all of us to fit in.

When my eyes open, the gold pearl is back up again, illuminating the sky. I go for a quick morning stroll.

We hadn't come to the urban part of Colzieu. The city is full of greenery. A small river is flowing by my side. It is the perfect city to live in. After this war is over, if we miraculously survive, Kelly, Archie, Andy, and I could live here.

As I walk, a newspaper floats in the wind and hits my head. I open it. The front page catches my eye.

Then I remember…

Awful

Ugly

Bad

Exhausting

Ruthless

Fearless

Obnoxious

Rude

Tiger

How was I so stupid? It is pretty obvious in the clue!

Clutching the paper in one hand, I sprint back.

"Guys! Guys! Get the car running. We're going to Auberfort," I shout from outside.

"What? Why?" Kelly asks.

"I will tell you on the way." I jump on.

When we are in mid-air, I start telling them why the change of plan. The front page of the newspaper tells us that Zephyr lied.

It read:

Sportsman is back for part 2!

The sportsman and masked man's fight at Glazenia seems to have a part 2. Several bombs were planted at public places like the mall and theatre, killing millions of people.

Right before sunrise, on the 19th of July, the sportsman was sighted in Auberfort. He was wearing black clothes. He seemed ready for war. He was fully armed with a vast army ready to fight for him. Was the sportsman going to fight with the masked man? Or was he planning to battle with someone else? Had he come to war? Or had he come to bomb Auberfort?

Around two years ago, the sportsman had fought a man wearing a mask for reasons unknown. The masked man had created a scar right across the sportsman's face. It is believed that the sportsman may be back for revenge.

Now that he is villainously planting bombs, it is difficult to tell if he or the masked man was innocent in the previous fight. Or are they both guilty? It is impossible to know! Why exactly is the sportsman getting into wars? What is the bigger picture? Unanswered questions appear like a mist hanging in the air.

See page 2.

"He lied. He came a day early. He was meant to come on the 20th, but instead, he came on the 19th," Alassia booms. "How did we not expect that?"

"On top of that, he is in Auberfort!" Fenna whines.

"A for *Awful,* U for *Ugly*, B for *Bad*, E for *Exhausting*, R for *Ruthless*, F for *Fearless*, O for *Obnoxious*, R for *Rude*, T for *Tiger*. A-U-B-E-R-F-O-R-T. Auberfort," I say, explaining the clue.

"When we reach, we need to be very careful. Zephyr could be anywhere," Kelly warns.

Finally, we are on top of Auberfort, descending steadily. Because it is late at night, there are rare chances of Zephyr seeing us. When the car touches the ground, we quietly get out. As sneakily as possible, we get into the nearest hotel. Before we could get in though, a dark voice comes from the mist.

"Well, well, well. Look who it is. Where are you going?" Zephyr asks.

No, I am not in a position to battle right now!

"We were looking for you," I say.

"Funny, I was searching for you," he says.

"Good luck at war, buddy. You will need it," Franz says.

"I see you have survived, Kelly and Danica! How is Master Ed? Oh right, he is dead," Zephyr taunts. "If you want, you can say hello to him in a matter of minutes. Tell him I miss him as well."

"Don't worry, you can call dibs on meeting him first, I can fulfil your wish," I tease.

"We will see."

"Hey, you wanna see some cool stunts?" he asks.

He doesn't wait for an answer. Straight away, he sends death strikes at the buildings near us.

"How was that?"

"Coo—" I punch Franz in the hand as he tries to compliment Zephyr. "Ouch!"

"That was cruel, especially the fact that you destroyed a whole building with hundreds of people in it!" I say, crossed arms.

"You can admit that it is pretty cool!"

"What if it isn't?"

"I can't do anything about it, then."

Suddenly, I feel some sort of vibrations on the ground.

"What was that?" I ask. "Is it an earthquake?"

"No, it isn't."

I see a giant shadow. I turn around. Before I know it, there are orange flames, ash, and smoke everywhere. A dragon blasted fire at us. Lucky for me, I am immune to fire. However, everyone else looks like they are in a toaster, all covered in ash, their hair standing tall, and they all have turned black — even Andy and Archie's red hair looks black now.

"Were you in the toaster recently?" I ask.

"Oh my god, that burns! Danica, water! Make it cold!" Alassia yelps.

"Okay." I throw some ice-cold water at them. "How's that?" I ask.

"Ahh!"

The dragon's body is beige. Its wide, daring eyes are staring in our direction. Its long wings are turmeric in colour. Its blood-coated, pointy teeth are ready to swallow us whole.

"Look out," I shriek.

They duck rapidly as the dragon exhales more fire at us.

"Close one."

I turn to Zephyr.

"Is he yours?" I ask.

He nods, grinning.

Ugh! Isn't it cool when your opponent has a giant dragon and you have nothing big? Nope, it is horrible. It feels like we are ants. Something tells me there are things way worse than a dragon waiting for us. Way worse.

I turn back to the dragon. Again, it shoots fire at us. If only I could tape its mouth. We dodge a couple of more times.

I turn some water into an ice spear. With enormous force, I throw it at the dragon. Cherry-red blood drips. It roars. As it roars, it breathes more fire. I am seriously getting tired of this dragon.

Full of courage, the dragon miraculously spewed more fire, risking the chance of it getting hit again. I try a few more spears. At last, it finally makes its final roar. Alas, it falls to the ground. Strangely, I feel a slight tingle of pity.

I turn around to face Zephyr. Oh, the look on his face! A once-in-a-lifetime opportunity. His eyes are wide. A droplet of sweat runs down his head. He is terror-stricken. The way he shifts his looks from me to the dragon looks like he is telling himself, *If this girl can beat a dragon with only her water powers, she being a guardian would make defeating me a piece of cake.*

I am pretty sure he knows he is immortal, but I think I stunned him so much that he forgot about it. Or he thinks I am so powerful, I can break through his immortality.

"War is tomorrow, right?" he asks, trying to cover up his fear. "I'll see you there. Bye!" He leaves, sprinting away on cheetah legs.

We all chuckle once he is gone.

"Oh my gosh, his face was hilarious. He looked like *he* was scared of...*me*!" I giggle. "Do I have monstrous teeth? Do I have wide spooky eyes?"

"What a coward," Franz says.

"Well, we better get some rest if we want to fight well tomorrow," Kelly says.

"Where exactly are we sleeping?" I ask.

Kelly looks at me in a way that discomforts me.

"No! No, no, no, no, no!" I whine, "I am not sleeping in the car. The seat is not soft."

"You can sleep on the street then. We will just go to the car," she says.

"Ugh!"

I try to get some sleep, but I can't stop thinking about tomorrow. I need rest. I need to sleep. I won't be able to fight tomorrow if I am not well-rested. I am going to war against an immortal dude and a girl, who can control my thoughts and easily make me give her the fraction of immortality I have from Master Ed. Even after processing all that, I manage to get a minute of sleep when Kelly wakes me up again.

"Come on," she whispers. "We need to go and find Zephyr before he finds us."

"Do we have to go now? I just fell asleep." I whine.

"Wake everyone else," Kelly says.

"Guys, wake up," I whisper.

"We're awake," Azteque says.

"Let's go!" I say.

-17-

War Begins

Franz tries finding Zephyr through his powers. We help by following Zephyr's footprints from last night when he made a run after being frightened by us. The footprints almost faded away probably since several hours have passed. They lead to a dead end near an abandoned building. The building is hoary, blemished, and cut in half. No doubt, it was one of Zephyr's victims.

"I don't think he is in there, let's turn back," Franz says.

"No harm trying," I say.

"Do we have to go there?" Davian complains.

"Coming?" I ask, walking towards the building.

They follow.

I have to say, I am not as brave about going into that abandoned building as I pretend to be. After finding out that I am destined to become the guardian, I think I have been trying to show leadership in the group. We go in.

Inside looks more unappealing than the outside. It is dusky. It seems the building can collapse at any moment. The walls are as dirty as a dumpster. The atmosphere is like an out-of-limits desert. There are cobwebs all around. Dust is in the air, and I cannot stop coughing. The only reason no one is asking me why I am crying is because everyone has dust in their eyes.

Though everything is disturbing in this building, the most disturbing thing is one of the clocks. The wall has so many broken, jammed, and non-functioning clocks, but one of them is still working perfectly fine. It is still ticking. The hands are still moving. Also, it is a grandfather clock, and the pendulum is swinging from left to right to left to right to… you get what I mean.

I take a closer look. Maybe I'll ask Andy and Archie to check out the mechanisms.

"Andy, Archie, come here for a second," I call. "How is this clock still working? No, sorry. Scratch that. *Why* is this clock still working?"

"Let me have a look," Andy says, taking the clock down from the wall. He turns it around and checks the batteries.

"This is not possible! These batteries are rusted. How can it be working? Unless…" Archie says.

"Unless it is working by magic," Andy suggests.

"Magic?" I ask.

"No one else can have magical powers except for Zephyr, Lezabel, and us. We're on the right track," Kelly says. She takes a look at the wall. She glares at it as if struck by an idea.

"What is it?" I ask.

"The outline of the clock is on the wall. No one needs to outline a clock unless they need to find their secret hideout. It might be the same reason why Zephyr might have gotten this clock to work. It might be to make this clock stand out from the other clocks," she says.

"Are you saying this outline of a clock leads to his hideout?" I ask. "You're really good at interpreting!"

"So, how does this work?" Fenna asks.

"I haven't figured out that part yet."

"Maybe we need to push this down?" Archie suggests.

I push it. It falls down and leaves a hole in the wall. On the other side is an empty room that looks cleaner and more intact.

"Huh? That was easy," I say.

I jump in, and everyone else follows.

Just as it appeared from the outside, the inside is an empty room with nothing in it. I walk around.

"This can't be his hideout. Can it?" I ask. "I was thinking there would be all of his weapons, monsters and — ahh!"

The tile I am standing on slides open, letting me fall down a deep hole. As I am falling, I accidentally pull a lever, causing the tile above me to close.

I couldn't have landed at a better time than this. Everyone is sleeping — snoring actually — which makes me lucky. No one wakes up by the loud thud of my crash land. Wow! That makes me really lucky.

I hear a scream coming from the hole. Entering the scene is Kelly. Another scream enters my ears. Andy and Archie. Followed by everyone else. They all stack themselves on me.

"Mind getting off me?" I whisper.

"Where are we?" Andy asks, a little too loudly.

"Shh!"

"Sorry!"

"Shh!"

I take my chance to look around. This place must be the bedroom. When I see Lezabel sleeping, an idea hits my mind.

"If I could get Lezabel to touch my mole while she is asleep and transfer her powers, it would be easier than trying to do it during the war," I say.

"Good idea," Kelly agrees.

Slowly and steadily, I move closer. Lezabel's hand is sticking outside the bed, making it easier for me to grasp it. I level my hand enough for her to touch me. I can only get one shot at this; I have to do this right the first time. Without hesitation, I put my arm forward, letting her thumb touch my mole. I keep it in that position. According to the few tests we had done before, a glow is meant to appear. I wait. Five seconds. Ten seconds. Fifteen seconds. I am close to quitting.

Please work. Please work. I make a silent prayer in my mind.

Impatient, my mind wrestles within itself. Should I keep waiting or should I give up? I am on the verge of stopping when something sparkles. Yes. The glow appears. Considering, I am about to go to war in a few seconds, having a smile on my face is bizarre.

Before anything else, I need to hide because Lezabel might wake up at any moment. I follow everyone into another room. Is that the animal room? It seems like it.

There is a Fotigris — no, two Fotigrises (Is that the plural of Fotigris?) — giving us a look that can only mean, *You're those girls who killed my daddy! Wait till I get back at you!*

There is a hydra. Another dragon roars fire as we pass. Some weird monster that has a lion's head, a bull's horn, a tiger's body, a leopard's — no, cheetah's — legs, and a snake for the tail (I think it is called a Polyzoo) gives us a perplexed look that might mean, *Hey, you're not one of the people working for Zephyr, are you?*

There are more animals — the most peculiar (some of which I haven't even heard of), making nasty faces as we pass by them. A few of the animals mind their own business. The only animals that are lacking are the phoenix and the Pegasus — thankfully, I won't have to kill them.

"Hey, Danica, why not give the new powers a try?" Franz suggests looking at the animals.

"Good idea!" I say, excited to bring Lezabel's telepathic power to test.

I look carefully at a large serpent. Is that a basilisk? Should I not be looking away from the basilisk instead of focusing directly on it? Actually, am I not immortal? Ha! Zephyr really thought that a basilisk could kill me! What a loser! I try to control it. With as much effort as I can manage to gather, I make it come to the good side.

As I am doing it, I get second thoughts. Should I be doing this? Is this the right thing to do? Do I really want to force the animals into joining our side instead of Zephyr's? Making up my mind, I release the basilisk to choose a side out of its own free will.

"Why did you do that?" Franz asks.

"Which part? The part where I controlled the basilisk, the part where I released the basilisk, or the part where I am about to punch your face?" I ask.

"The part where you're about to punch me in the face and the part where you release the weird snake thingy," he says.

"Basilisk," I correct.

"Whatever, balisiks—"

"Basilisk."

"My point, dear young girl, is that we were so close to having the balisisk in our clutches," he complains.

"Basilisk. Also, is it really what you want? To have to control the basilisk to make it come to us? Shouldn't the basilisk get to choose for itself? Whether it is right or wrong, the basilisk should have its chance to make a choice."

"Gee, Miss Lecture Queen!"

"Call me Lecture Queen again, and I will punch you real hard."

"Lecture Quee… Ouch! What was that for?"

"For calling me Lecture Queen! Told you I'd punch."

"Lecture Queen!"

"You're so lucky I only gave you a punch, I could do way worse," I warn.

"How worse?" he asks.

"Tornado worse!"

"Will you guys be quiet?" Kelly interrupts.

We move on. The next room is full of weapons. Bows and arrows, spears, harpoons, etc. There are a lot of weapons, too many to count.

We go into the following room. There is a plan in this one. The one room I was waiting for. The room is filled with writing, sketches, and diagrams. We grab everything and start reading. Normally, reading is not my thing, but on this occasion, it has to be. I skim through the writing to get a brief idea of their plan.

"According to the papers I am reading, they have no idea how I am going to steal any of their powers," I whisper.

"Not in mine either," Kelly says.

"Good," I say. "Speaking of powers, why am I not stealing Zephyr's powers?"

"Probably because Zephyr sleeps consciously. He'd wake up easily, which leaves us in danger," Kelly says. "Also, you already have immortality. You can't take away Zephyr's powers until you're the guardian. You aren't the guardian until you have all nine powers. Clear?"

"As day."

I try finding some more papers with useful information.

I notice a piece of paper on the wall. *Ah, that seems helpful.*

When I snatch it off, I notice a strange dot engraved on the wall. The dot itself isn't strange, but what's strange is why it is there. I touch the dot. Nothing. I push the brick backwards. The brick falls and makes a loud thud on the other side as it crash-lands, revealing a box. The reason I am curious is that there must be something important in the box. Zephyr wouldn't go through so much trouble to hide a bunch of nonsense behind a wall. Just as I am about to open the box, I hear a familiar voice.

"Snooping, are we? Are you children that I need to teach you manners? Right. Yes, you are. So, how about we start with this? Prying is bad manners," Zephyr tells.

"In that case, we 'children' know more about manners than you do. After all, you're a rude, mean, and selfish man. Next time you try teaching us a lesson, make sure you don't do the same things," I say.

I try to focus inside his brain. Please work. I need to know what is going on in his mind. After a while, I hear Zephyr whispering inside my head. *The death strike ought to weaken them, if not kill them.*

Yes! It worked. Now, I need to try to stop him from doing the death strike.

He lifts his hand getting ready to zap. I focus on his mind again. This time, instead of gaining knowledge, I control his mind to zap himself. Forcefully, he points his hand towards himself.

What is happening? he asks himself. *Why am I zapping myself?*

Within three seconds, something black comes out of his fingers, straight at his heart.

"Ouch!" He screams, bending with agony.

He gets up again. He glances at me, wide-eyed. I grin at him. He gives the same terrified look he had given me last night.

"Hahaha! You just zapped yourself. Do you hate yourself now?" I ask.

"That was not funny. How did you do that?" he asks.

"Are you expecting me to reveal my secret to my archnemesis?" I ask. "Sure. I stole Lezabel's powers! Cool, isn't it?"

"You what? How?" he asks.

"That is a secret I am not at all telling you. Figure it out yourself. I'll leave you to it," I say, walking out the door.

When I am outside, I stop in my tracks. Everyone stops with me.

"What is wrong?" Kelly asks.

"We need to burn down that place!"

"How?" Davian asks.

"Last time I checked, Alassia didn't mind being a dragon," I say.

"I still don't," she says, already a dragon.

She turns towards the room and breathes enough fire for the room to go up in flames.

She shapeshifts back into a human, and we start walking for the exit.

Obviously, I cannot expect nobody to stop us from escaping. When we reach the room we had come from, I see a large group of combat faces led by Lezabel. We get ready to charge. Before anyone can even shout battle cries, Zephyr comes in and utters three words.

"Let them go."

Everyone stops, stunned. We all look at each other, confused.

"What?" Lezabel asks.

"What?" Franz asks.

"Let them go," Zephyr repeats. "We aren't prepared, Lezabel. Danica has your powers. We need a change of plan."

"Are you afraid you will lose?" I demand.

"No. We're merely not ready!"

"I challenge you to fight us up in the streets!"

"What?" he asks.

"I challenge you to—"

"I heard what you said. I meant, now?" Zephyr says.

"Yes, right now. Why? Are you scared?" I ask.

"No! I was just… Ugh! Forget it. I accept the challenge," he says, pretending to show full courage.

"What?" Lezabel asks.

"What is up with everyone saying 'What?' " I ask

We go upstairs. Zephyr's team goes first, followed by us. We have to climb the hole we had come from, which, trust me, is not very easy. Honestly, it is harder than climbing a flat wall because the ice knives I poke into the sand keep slipping.

When we are up, we get out of the building. We stayed behind them the whole time till now, making sure they don't try to pull any tricks before we reach.

I, telepathically, send a message to Andy, and Archie to go back to the cars to hide. They do as I said. They try to sneak out. I cover for them by bending Lezabel and Zephyr's minds to not see them.

We get ourselves ready. I stand in front of my team; Zephyr stands in front of his. I look Zephyr in the eye. Even without recent mindpower add-ons, I could easily understand how petrified he is.

He starts with the attack. He attacks us with his death strike. No problem about that. I send my water towards him. He does get pushed to the ground, but that is after Kelly falls from his strike.

"Kelly, are you okay?" I ask.

"Yeah, yeah. I'm fine. Can I get a hand?" she asks, pulling out her hand.

I give her mine. She gets up, cracks a few knuckles, and smiles at me.

I get back to the war. Zephyr is literally the only one with powers on his side. This is going to be easy.

I use my mind power to make Zephyr jump into the pool in some rich guy's backyard. Seemingly, he can't swim. What a surprise! He tries to keep his nose above the surface.

I make a snake rise from the water. Slowly and steadily, it goes towards Zephyr. It stops right in front of Zephyr's face. Rapidly, it hits Zephyr in the heart. He falls into the pool. I make the snake twirl around Zephyr, grabbing him.

It makes Zephyr crash on the floor. Ouch. I almost feel like this is too cruel, but then I realise that there is no mercy in war. After about two minutes, I make the snake disappear, letting Zephyr sink.

I get back to the battle. I see Zephyr's army, led by Lezabel, fighting ferociously against my friends. I run quickly into battle, two water tentacles following me. My right hand controls the tentacle on my right, and my left hand controls the one on my left. I first target Lezabel. My right hand punches the air, facing Lezabel. The right tentacle follows my command and punches Lezabel. She falls to the ground. I make the tentacles punch her even more.

According to the plan, now is the time. I was supposed to take everyone's powers one by one, allowing me to gradually become more powerful while most of my friends retained their abilities to fight. According to my theory, they would need to press my mole a second time to grant immortality, as I doubt the first press transfers both their power and immortality.

I look at Franz. He looks back at me. With a reluctant look, he nods. I make one of the tentacles pull him closer to me. I give him a message, *I am so sorry, Franz.*

Franz puts his thumb on my mole. The glow doesn't come. Lezabel seems to be getting up.

Quick! Quick! Quick!

Lezabel sits up perfectly fine. Before Lezabel can notice what is going on, I send a message to everyone to cover for me. They manage to keep her away for quite some time, but still, nothing happens. No shimmer.

I decide it is best if we restart. He waits for two more seconds. Nothing. It is pointless. He takes his thumb off. Just as he takes it off, I see a glint of light. *Did it work?*

I try to see what is inside the nearest building. I can't. I try harder. I see a party going on in one of the houses. *Is it a birthday party?* Nonetheless, that pretty much makes it clear that I did get Franz's powers.

Having Lezabel captured is too easy. Kelly simply drew a cage and dropped it behind Lezabel. Alassia turned into a dragon and scared her in. There, she is captured.

But, something doesn't feel right about this. Nothing is too easy.

Unexpectedly, a death strike comes straight at us, forcing us to the ground.

When I next open my eyes, I am lying on the ground, and Zephyr is standing next to Lezabel. Everyone is crowded around Franz. I get up to check what is going on.

Franz doesn't move a muscle. I try shaking him. His heart isn't beating. He isn't breathing either. No, my theory was wrong. I was wrong. His immortality came along with the rest of his powers.

"Oh no! This is all my fault," I snivel.

"Don't be stupid. How can this be your fault?" Kelly asks.

"I am the one who took away his powers. I must have taken his immortality as well," I sob.

"If anyone is to blame, it's Zephyr. If he hadn't blown that stupid black lightning of his, no one would have died," Fenna cries.

"If I hadn't made him drown, he wouldn't have had the motivation to do so," I complain.

"Stop blaming yourself. It isn't going to make things any better," Kelly says.

"For Franz's sake, we've to kill Zephyr," I say.

"Let's make sure he didn't die for no reason," Fenna says.

This time, Fenna leads. I am too depressed by Franz's death to fight. I am expecting Fenna to send lightning to Zephyr directly. But instead, she decides to do something cleverer. She sends lightning to Zephyr through a bow and arrow. She secretly electrocutes the arrow. She aims at Zephyr and then releases. Zephyr steps to the right to dodge it. Just then, I send ice at him — at least that is what I meant to do. Instead of getting stuck in his arm, it misses. I can't concentrate at all.

To help make things better, while Zephyr is too distracted, laughing at my miss, Fenna shoots lightning at Zephyr. The good thing about lightning is that it is the fastest thing on Earth. However, Franz's death got into our time traveller's head, too. Davian wasn't concentrating properly, so instead of slowing Zephyr down, he sped him up, allowing him to dodge the lightning. The lightning misses him by merely a centimetre.

I send Alassia a message to turn into a helpful creature like a dragon. Instead, she turns into a turtle that looks like it is wearing a dragon costume. She tries turning back but only manages to turn into a purple-coloured pigeon. She soon ends up turning into random animals having random colours, instead of turingn back into the human form. She is too agitated to do so.

Fenna turns into a piece of burnt toast. The only thing she has managed to do is electrocute herself.

Lezabel and Zephyr dodge anything we put at them, which I am not surprised considering how badly we are fighting. Is it even possible for karate to win in karate vs. powers? Well, now it is. While Zephyr just stands in the corner, Lezabel is karate-ing us. She kicks my chest, punches Kelly, kicks Alassia and Fenna simultaneously. Oh, I wonder how she can do that? Six people with super cool and supernatural powers are off-sync against one girl with nothing but karate skills.

All of us are lying on the floor, struggling to get up. After great effort, I get up and give a hand to everyone else.

Spontaneously, I send ice toward Lezabel. She dodges. No, scratch that. She *almost* dodges. The ice gives her a scratch on her back, tearing her shirt. A red line appears. Lezabel tries not to scream, but she does release a soft yelp.

I get the feeling that we are missing someone. Where is Zephyr? I try looking for him.

Kelly draws a dragon. Alassia successfully turns into a dragon. An idea pops into my head. I try controlling the water, turning it into a dragon made of water. Fenna tries the same thing as me, creating a dragon made of lightning. We all command the dragons to run towards Lezabel. Right in front of her, the dragons breathe fire (though my dragon breathes water and Fenna's breathes lightning).

Lezabel tries her best to dodge, but this time my mindpower overpowers her. She gets set on fire, but the water from my dragon washes it off — how lucky she is to have me here — and the lightning from Fenna's dragon electrocutes her.

Lezabel is on the floor in her worst condition. We go over to check on her. Her body is more burnt than Zephyr's. If she survives that, it would be a miracle. No, don't think like that. She is like any other human. She can't survive. No chance.

As if to prove my point, Davian exclaims, "She isn't breathing. Her heart has stopped pumping."

When he says that, I feel a little sorry for her.

"Is that a good thing? I don't feel right about this. She hasn't killed anyone to deserve death. The only bad thing she has ever done is partnering with Zephyr. Also, doesn't this make us murderers?" I say.

Everyone's faces turn gloomy.

I hear the conversation going on between my heart and brain.

Heart: Danica has a point. Lezabel doesn't deserve to die.

Brain: Yes, she does. Think logically! She has been controlling us to do things we dislike.

Heart: She isn't a murderer, though.

Brain: She is a witch.

Heart: We are way worse than her. We have gone as far as killing. She hasn't done anything to us.

Brain: You are being stupid. You are the good one. She is the bad one.

Heart: I still think this was a terrible thing to do.

"I can't believe we just did that," Davian says.

"I think I know how we can set things right though," I say.

"How?" Azteque asks.

"We revive her," I suggest.

"Oh, goddess of stupidity, Danica, reviving the dead is impossible," Kelly says.

"O, goddess of know-it-all, Kelly, reviving the dead is possible!" I say. "I remember, two years ago, when I had been killed by one of Zephyr's guards, I was revived later by Zephyr himself."

"Why would he revive you?" Azteque asks.

"Because he didn't want to search for the water girl all over again," I say.

"How did he revive you?" Kelly asks.

"I think the person with immortality has the power of reviving anyone from the dead."

"You mean, any of us can revive her?" Fenna says.

"It is that easy?" Azteque asks. "Okay then, I will go and revive her."

He opens his palm and turns it toward Lezabel's body. Nothing happens. He tries focusing.

"It isn't working," he complains.

"Try harder and focus," I say.

He keeps trying. "Still nothing!"

"Let me try." I push him aside.

I widen my palm, and turning it toward Lezabel, I focus as hard as possible. It isn't working!

"Why won't it work?" I wonder.

"Maybe you aren't good enough! Let me try," Kelly says.

While she is pointlessly trying it herself, I get an idea.

"What if we all try together? Our immortality anyways is just several pieces from Master Ed. If we fix them together, we make a whole."

We gather around Lezabel. Everyone widens their hand. Still, nothing happens.

"Maybe we could use our second arm to touch the person to our left. Like how puzzle pieces need to touch each other to form the whole picture," I say.

We touch each other with our left hand. After a few seconds, white lightning strikes at Lezabel, continuously. The lightning stops automatically after a minute. We pull back our hands. Hoping she would move, we stare at her.

She doesn't move at all. Breaking the suspense, dark lightning shoots right next to us. We turn around.

"What are you doing with her?" Zephyr appears out of nowhere and asks, shooting more death strikes at us.

"Nothing," I say.

Zephyr pushes through.

When he sees Lezabel, he gives us a daring look.

"You killed her!" He booms.

"We also revived her," Davian says.

"Why should I believe you?" he asks.

Lezabel coughs.

"Heard that?" Azteque asks.

Zephyr takes another look at Lezabel. She sits up straight. It worked!

I send a message to everyone, *You guys know what he is like when he gets angry. It is better if we leave.*

How? Kelly wonders.

Steam.

I spill water on the floor underneath us. I have never done this before, but it is worth a try. Steam will help create a distraction for Zephyr and he won't be able to see anything through it. I heat up the water. It starts to steam like hot water in a bubble bath. Since I have an amazing sight now, I gather everyone. Everyone including Franz.

Azteque, teleport us.

He takes us to the flying cars again.

-18-

Hypno-locket

Everyone stares at Franz solemnly. Tears flow down our eyes.

"Wait a second!" Davian says, a little too excited for the current mood. "We can revive Franz like we revived Lezabel," he suggests.

"Man," Azteque says, "you're a genius!"

I could see a faint tingle of hope in everyone. We all stand around Franz. Just like earlier, we touch our left hand to the person next to us, so we are connected, and we hold out an open fist. Again, lightning comes, and goes after some time.

We wait patiently. By patiently, I mean…

"When is he coming alive?" Fenna asks.

"He should be alive by now! Why isn't he waking up?" I scream in agitation. Yes. Patiently.

Suddenly, I hear his breathing. He coughs. A large smile appears on my face. On everyone's face. With immense joy, I hug Franz.

"We did it," I cry.

"Yes, we did it," Kelly says.

Everyone is beaming at Franz.

"I am back guys," Franz exclaims.

"Yes, you are," Kelly says.

The relief in me is something I cannot explain. My heart is filled with contentment and glee. It is impossible for the smile on my face to wear off.

"Franz," I realise, "you aren't immortal. You can die easily."

"Oh right," Franz says.

"How about you don't enter war tomorrow?" I suggest.

"No way. You need me," he says.

"I know we do, but this is for your own good," I say.

Franz reluctantly agrees.

"When we go off to war tomorrow, you find a good place to hide and stay there. And take my brothers with you too. Okay?" I ask.

"Okay."

When the sun sets, we eat dinner. Kelly cooks (I mean, draws) a delicious meal for us. When we are done with the feast, and our food is digested, we go to sleep.

The next morning, I am woken up — this time, not by Kelly, but by Zephyr. He hits his death strike at the car we are in, breaking it. The loud noise of his black lightning startles me awake. Thankfully, nothing hits Franz or my brothers. I send Franz a message telling him to hide somewhere. I control Zephyr's mind to make him think that Franz, Andy, and Archie are not there. They go out of the car and into the nearest building.

I hit Zephyr with a few ice balls, a few larger ice balls, and a few massive boulder-size ice balls. All they give to Zephyr are a few bruises. Zephyr keeps striking at us. We first get out of the car so we have enough space to dodge. We dodge every attack of Zephyr.

He strikes at a building behind as. Breaking into half, a part of it falls onto us. We end up crushed flat on the ground. Ow! We try pushing the building up. Obviously, all of us added together are still not strong enough to lift a building. Azteque touches the building with his right palm. He cleverly teleports it to the part of the sky above Zephyr. The building falls down at Zephyr, squishing him just like it did to us.

Zephyr stays squished in there for ages. That is when Lezabel comes in. She has a locket around her neck. She goes in front of Azteque,opens the locket and puts it right in front of his eyes. Azteque looks away but Lezabel chases his eyeballs. Even Azteque is aware that something bad can happen by simply looking at that locket. At one point, the locket catches his eye. He straightens himself as if waiting for a command.

Lezabel whispers, "Teleport that building over there."

"Yes, Queen Lezabel!"

"Hahaha!" She chuckles at the word *Queen*.

Azteque does as he is told. The building teleports towards Zephyr's right. Zephyr stands up. He bends backwards to make his back feel better. His whole body turns tomato-red.

Zephyr is about to shoot another death strike at us, but I manage to freeze him into ice before he can. He stands frozen, while Lezabel plans her next move. I know exactly what she is going to do now.

She comes over to me. Before she can even manage to show me her locket, I knock her down with ice.

"Don't mess with me," I threaten, "and don't you ever *dare* hypnotise me."

As a little joke, I make her say, "Yes, Queen Danica."

"Hahaha! Now, who's the one laughing?" I chuckle.

Zephyr uses his death strike to break the ice. His hair stands tall. He tries moving, but he is too cold to move. He shivers while lying on the spot.

Getting bored of watching him shiver, Fenna zaps him with lightning. He gets electrocuted, making him get energy again. Zephyr sends death strikes at us, one after the other. A slight part of the last strike hits us. We almost fall, but we regain balance. Zephyr strikes again. This time, we all hit the ground.

When I open my eyes, I see Zephyr using each of his fingers to strike at each person but me. The next thing I see is a swirly thing. Isn't that a locket? No, it is *the* locket — Lezabel's hypnotism locket. I stand up straight. Zephyr stops striking at Fenna, while Lezabel hypnotises her as well. One by one she hypnotises each of us. We all stand up, waiting for a command.

After a few seconds, Lezabel utters the most dangerous words, "Give your power to Zephyr."

I try fighting the command but the spell seems strong. I use mind control to stop everyone from giving the powers, but Lezabel's spell seems to beat it. Slowly, I walk forward, trying to turn back. If Zephyr gets all the powers, he becomes the guardian. When I am in front of Zephyr, I am wrestling with the spell.

'Don't do this,' I tell myself.

'Do this!' the spell tells me.

The spell's words overpowered mine, making me touch Zephyr's mole. The glow appears. The second my power is his, I am able to control myself. Defeated, I move aside.

When everyone is done, Zephyr snickers, "I am now the guardian! Something I had been waiting to be for centuries. No one can stop me now!"

"Ahh!" Davian screams.

"Chill, it's not like it is the end of the world," Azteque says.

"It is," Davian yells.

"Tell me, former Revenirs, how do you feel?" Zephyr asks.

We don't reply.

"You know, with these amazing powers, first of all, I am going to start killing you guys," he says.

He uses his shape-shifting power to transform into a dragon. He exhales fire at us. Everyone, but me, gets burnt. Nothing happens to me. Wait what? How is that possible? I can't still be immune to fire, can I? Maybe it is because I used to have water powers. Even Zephyr looks stunned.

"How? How? How is that possible? You guys should be dead, and, you should at least be burnt, Danica. You can't still be immune to fire, can you?" he asks.

"Who knows? Maybe I still have my water powers," I say. Though I don't think so. "Lezabel's locket is probably too weak."

Zephyr tries to send ice at me. Nothing. He tries controlling the water. Still nothing. He looks at Lezabel.

"You're doing it wrong. It is like this," I say. Not expecting what the outcome would be, I show him how to control water. What! How? The water obeys my command.

"No way! You clearly gave me your power," Zephyr complains. When he says power, I realise something.

"You see, that is where you're correct. I did give you my power — without an 's'. That means I gave you one power out of the three kinds of powers I had. Clearly, the water power isn't the one I gave you. Besides, you already have immortality, which means you can't take our immortality unless you become the guardian. Haha!" I tell.

"Does this mean he isn't the guardian?" Kelly asks.

"Yes, it does," I exclaim. "It also means that getting all the powers is going to be easy, now that they're in one place."

"What power do I have?" Zephyr wonders.

He tries controlling me to give him all my powers. It doesn't work.

"I don't have mind control," he says, disappointed. "That means I've boring supervision."

I control his mind to come to me and give me his powers. He tries to block it, but I overpower him. He slowly comes towards me. When he is three metres away, Lezabel cuts through. She puts the locket in front of Zephyr. I try to cover the locket with my hand. Too late, he already caught a glimpse of the spiral.

Zephyr stops and waits for a command. What if I say the command? Would it still work?

Before Lezabel can open her mouth anything, I say, "Give Danica your *powers*."

"Yes, Queen Lezabel."

Why did he say Queen Lezabel? It is probably part of the spell. Zephyr continues walking toward me. When he is two metres away, Lezabel blocks his way. I push Lezabel away. Zephyr comes closer to me. Before he touches my mole, Lezabel dives onto him, pushing him aside.

"You will not go to Danica!" she commands.

Obviously, she isn't using her locket this time, which means Zephyr is still keen on giving me his powers.

He struggles, trying to release himself from Lezabel's grasp. He punches Lezabel and kicks her. He almost decides to hit her with a death strike. While fighting Zephyr, Lezabel loses grip of her locket. Before she can take it back, I go closer to her and snatch it away.

Lezabel loses concentration and ends up letting Zephyr come after me. While he is marching towards me, I control some ice to break the locket. Right before he touches my mole, he realises what he is doing. He moves back.

"Why did he not touch my mole?" I ask.

"Because you broke it, stupid!" Lezabel grins.

I look at the broken locket. What a big mistake.

Zephyr grins at me. "Thanks a lot. If not for your dumbness, all the powers I have would be yours."

"You wait. The powers will be mine," I say.

Before I can do anything, Zephyr hits a big death strike.

The next time I wake up, I don't see Zephyr or Lezabel anywhere. The others are surrounding me, waiting for me to wake up.

Once I straighten up, we go find Franz and the others.

"Franz?" I scream.

"Andy?" Kelly says.

"Archie?" Fenna shouts.

"We're here," Franz screams back from the building to our right.

We reach there quickly.

"I saw everything. It didn't seem nice," Franz says.

"I am tired now. I think everyone else is too. We should take some rest," Davian says.

"Well, the car is broken. Where do we sleep?" I ask.

"There are sofas in the nearby hotel lobby. I saw a few people sleeping there," Andy says.

"Okay," I say, yawning.

We enter the building. Wow! It looks so rich. The diamond chandelier is glimmering. The glossy marble floor, the soft pink sofas look so elegant and classy. I jump onto the sofa and fall asleep immediately.

I am quite surprised that I even managed to get some sleep. These days, however tired I am, I can't sleep very easily. Today is different.

-19-

Guardian

I am the first to wake up. I go outside to watch the night sky. The sun hasn't even come up yet. Glimmering like a silver pearl, the bright moon is floating in the sky. The stars, like silver glitter, are gleaming in the sky. Hours pass. Slowly, the sky starts to change colour as the sun comes up. It is a gradient of navy blue and sunrise orange. A faint part of the sun is touching the horizon.

After half an hour, Kelly comes out.

"You're awake?" She whispers.

"Woke up in the middle of the night. Couldn't sleep again," I reply.

"Oh."

"How did you know I am outside?" I ask.

"Saw you through the window."

She walks back in.

"Guys, wake up! We don't want a surprise attack by Zephyr," she whispers.

"I'm awake," Franz says and then continues snoring.

"Franz!"

"Okay! Now, I am wide awake," he declares, still yawning.

When everyone is awake, I say, "I don't think anyone should come. You all don't have any powers!"

"We still have immortality. We can't die," Kelly says.

"Oh, right."

We go out of the lobby. Andy, Archie, and Franz stay back. We start walking randomly until we bump into Zephyr.

Before I can get ready to attack, Zephyr shoots his death strike at me. When I fall down and lie unconscious, he grabs my arm. Without hesitation, he makes my index finger touch his mole. While waiting for the glow, Lezabel occupies everyone else. The glow doesn't come for about five minutes.

My eyes finally open, and I realise what is happening. Immediately, I remove my hand before the glow comes.

"I swear I had you there," Zephyr complains.

"Well, now you don't," I say, sending a water tentacle at him.

I wrap the tentacle around him and turn it into ice. He stays stuck. I make his finger touch my mole. He doesn't try to stop me. I realise why. Just after he touches it, he performs the death strike on my mole. If someone performs the death strike on a Revenir mole, it is hard to explain the kind of intense pain the Revenir goes through. You have to experience it to understand.

"Ahh!" I cry in agony.

The mole stings so bad, I cannot even express it. Gradually, it starts stinging the skin surrounding the mole. The prickle is eventually spreading to my whole body. Kelly comes after me.

"What happened, Danica?" she asks.

"Death strike…mole…stings," I say, hardly able to speak.

"We'll cover for you," Fenna suggests.

"Please…do," I manage to say.

They turn to Zephyr.

"Boys, take Lezabel. We will take Zephyr," Fenna says.

The girls, without powers, punch and kick Zephyr enough to make him fall down. Since when did they learn to do karate so well? Zephyr gets up again and shoots a few strikes at them. Luckily, their powers were the only things gone, not immortality.

They jump back up and get into karate mode. Unfortunately, Zephyr's death strike is way stronger than karate. Seeing my friends getting constantly shot by the death strike while I sit back and relax is a terrible sight to witness — the worst, I must say.

When I feel like the pain is in the process of completely walking away, I get up and help. First, I slap Zephyr a few hundred times with a water tentacle. I wrap the tentacle around him and lift him 50 feet up in the air. Zephyr looks green. He seems to be on the verge of puking. Ew. Gross. He closes his eyes, trying not to look down. When he does look down, he resists the urge to yelp.

"Someone's scared of heights," I say.

The tentacle releases him, allowing him to free-fall to his death — well, maybe not death. Remember, he is immortal. He screams like he is about to die, which he isn't. How can *he* be scared of heights? He crash-lands on his head. With his head crashed, I hope he loses his memory or his brain gets reset, because that would mean the war is over. Sadly, that is the most unlikely thing to happen; I am not that lucky!

Zephyr lies unconscious on the floor. I swear I heard a crack from the neck. Must have been his bone. Everyone does their karate on Lezabel, while I handle the whole becoming a guardian thing. I get Zephyr to touch my mole. I wait. Behind me, my friends are trying to stop Lezabel from reaching me or Zephyr. I keep shifting looks from Zephyr's eyes — please don't wake up — to the mole — please glow.

After 10 seconds, Zephyr slowly opens his eyes. When he sees me in front of him, he almost blows the death strike at me until something stuns him. The glow appears. At last, I am about to be the guardian of the Revenirs.

"No! No! No! No! No!" he screams, trying to shoot a death strike in his rage.

"I did it," I exclaim with joy. "We did it!"

I turn to my friends. When I turn back, Zephyr is nowhere to be seen.

"Coward," I mutter. We walk back to that luxurious hotel lobby.

Before we do anything, I manipulate the staff's mind to think that we aren't there.

"Now is a good time to start. Who's first?" I ask.

Kelly rests her thumb on my hand. In a few seconds, the glow appears. After giving her immortality to me, she neither seems sad nor happy. I guess she doesn't care if her immortality is gone.

Davian puts his thumb next, with an expression that looks in between 'I don't care' and 'I am heartbroken'. He quickly gets it over with.

On a scale from 1-10, Azteque's sadness of giving up immortality is 100. "I will miss you, immortality! I will," he says.

Franz and my brothers just sit back, watching Azteque on the verge of tears. I feel Azteque is getting overdramatic. Franz pats Azteque on the back to comfort him.

When there is just one person left, we expect a brighter glow, or something different to happen. That's because when everyone has given me their immortality, I would become the guardian.

As a matter of fact, something extraordinarily brilliant happens. My whole body starts glowing. My insides feel purer. I feel fresh. I feel majestic — ah, that's the right word. Everyone glares at me with amazement.

"Wow!" they say.

The glow goes off in a minute.

"That...was...so... I am speechless," Fenna says.

"Marvellous, wow, magnifique, amazing, and countless other words!" Franz exclaims.

"It also feels great on the inside!" I tell.

"You're officially the guardian!" Kelly says.

"Though, I don't think I am going to keep these guardian powers," I say.

"Why not?" Franz asks.

"Because I don't want there to be any such thing as Revenirs. I don't want children like us going to war when they could be enjoying themselves with their friends," I say.

"Fair enough."

Being the guardian of the Revenirs is a huge deal. If I weren't so tired of this Revenir business, I would be celebrating my victory. However, victory isn't assured until I take Zephyr's powers once and for all. Speaking of which, how am I going to get all his powers? Master Ed had struggled, even when he had practised for millennials. What can I do?

"How do I get Zephyr's immortality?" I ask.

"It isn't going to be easy, that I can tell you," Fenna says.

"I've got an idea," Kelly exclaims.

She tells us her plan. It's clever. We decide to go hunting for Zephyr at dawn. I make sure to get some sleep instantly.

When it is first light, Kelly wakes me up. We set out. The horizon is the golden part of the navy-blue sky. Stars look like white paint sprinkled on a painting.

" Let's go to the place where we battled him. We can get clues from there," Franz suggests.

"Or, I could just use the fact that I am a guardian to sense where his magic is," I say.

"That could work, too," he says.

I try locating his magic. I get a slight sense.

"It seems to be coming all the way from the opposite side of Auberfort," I tell.

"Andy, Archie, can you whip up something for us to get there?" Franz asks.

"Sure," they say, already putting their brains to work.

"Or can't I just teleport us there?" I ask.

"Right."

Being quite familiar with how it works, everyone touches my arm. Andy and Archie just follow the rest. I snap my fingers. We are on a whole different side of Auberfort, in the rural lands. In front of us, there is a huge rock, the size of a building.

"The Great Rock," Kelly gasps.

"He is in there," I say.

If you have never been to The Great Rock, I apologise for the spoilers. We go closer to the rock. Thinking that she must have read about this rock somewhere, we follow Kelly's lead. She starts climbing the rock, so we just decide to follow. We hike up, till we reach the top. There is an entrance on the rock, at the top. We open it. When I look down, I see a dark tunnel, going straight downwards. One by one, we jump in.

Unlike all the other times I had fallen down (for example at the entrance to Zephyr's secret hideout before the war, the entrance to our secret training place in Alenzon, etc.), this time I crash on my head. I am 100% sure I jumped feet first. On the way down, I end up in a sitting position, with my legs stretched in front of me. Obviously, the tunnel isn't big enough to let me stay in that position, so I get stuck. To make matters worse, Franz falls onto my stomach. That makes my legs go higher and my torso even lower. Franz gets stuck with me, and pushes my head down, so that I am falling head first. Luckily, I don't hear even a crack of my bone. Unluckily — ow! — it hurts. Thanks a lot, Franz.

Around me, the place looks like we are inside a hollow rock — because we are. There is complete nothingness, and I see no sign of Zephyr. Where could he be?

"Let's check every inch of this place. He has to be here somewhere," I say.

Everyone goes searching. I check the walls for anything not ordinary. Nothing. I check the floor. Nothing. Wait, no. There's something! I see a square cut into the rock. I try pushing it down, but it won't budge. I try pulling it up. It is too heavy, but I manage to lift it open in the end. We jump down though the opening and land in a small space, this time on our feet. In the corner, I see Zephyr.

"Give me your powers, Zephyr," I order.

"Why should I?"

"Because I said so," I say.

"And, I am supposed to do what you say? Give up centuries of hard work for you?" he asks.

"If you don't give it to me, I guess I will have to make you."

I slowly make water cover Zephyr, leaving only an opening for me to touch his mole. He tries to zap me in the process with his death strike, but I quickly freeze his hands. Lezabel appears from nowhere and tries to push me, but one zap of lightning makes her drop to the ground. I walk over to Zephyr, savagely raise an eyebrow, and press my thumb against his mole. The glow appears.

Now, I have officially won. I have become the guardian and taken away Zephyr's powers. The best part: the look on Zephyr's face. He lost everything he had been working towards. It is unbelievable that two years ago, I was simply complaining about going to school. Oh boy, I have got to be grateful from now on.

I unfreeze Zephyr. The second I do, he tries to come after me, but I teleport all of us before he could reach us. We end up in a desert.

-20-

Dad

"Are we going to go our separate ways?" I ask everyone. "Now that everything is back to normal."

"Danica, Kelly, Andy and Archie, you all can come to my house. My parents wouldn't mind," Fenna suggests, realising that we, siblings have nowhere to go.

"Seems like a wonderful idea if your parents don't mind four extra kids to take care of, two of them being such annoying pests," I say, looking at my brothers.

"So, it's final?" Fenna asks.

"Thank you so much."

I teleport everyone to their respective cities. It was hard to say goodbye after having shared such an interesting adventure together.

Fenna leads us to her house. Turns out, Franz is her next-door neighbour!

Fenna gives us a tour of the house. It's gorgeous. She also shows us the guestrooms where we will stay.

We find Fenna's parents in their room, sleeping.

"Are they your parents?" I ask.

"Yes. Shh."

Her parents slowly open their eyes.

"Fenna?" Her dad asks, his lightning-blue eyes widening.

"Yes, Dad," Fenna blinks back tears.

I leave the room to allow Fenna and her parents some privacy. I go into the guest room and lie in bed. Today was a long day. I had finished the war. I can finally say that peace has come. Now, I can rest.

After I wake up from a peaceful power nap, Fenna calls us down for dinner. I go and sit at the table. An awkward silence lingers throughout the whole meal. No one utters a word. When we are done with our food, Fenna and I go for a walk. Kelly stays back and helps Fenna's father with the dishes, while my brothers go to their rooms.

"I still have incomplete tasks to do. I need to find my dad and kill him. Then, I will find the harp. Considering the harp gave powers to Master Ed, I am pretty sure I can put my powers back into it and break the harp."

"Oh. Right. But, just chill for the moment, all right?"

"But, I need to —"

"Chill."

"Fine."

We walk and talk for a while.

Suddenly, Fenna looks up. "Did you feel that?"

"Feel what?" I ask. Then, a droplet falls on my head. "Yes, I felt that."

"It is about to rain! We better go inside," Fenna says. "Can you —"

"Yes."

I make a fist, stopping the rain from coming onto us. We walk home, completely dry. We step into the house with not a droplet on us.

I go upstairs to my room, while Fenna goes to her parents' room to spend some time with them.

Oh, what I wouldn't give to be able to see my mom again. I wonder if my mom is in the dark place I went to or heaven. I bet she is in paradise, enjoying herself. I find myself smiling at that thought. Kelly and my brothers are the only family I have got now. I don't count my dad as 'family'.

I lie on my bed and try to think of places my dad could be. Should I start at the house we lived in before everything happened? It seems like the perfect place for him to be. I guess that's settled then, I will go check the house later today. Lying in bed, I am bound to fall asleep, which I do.

The next morning, I go to Fenna's parents to ask for clothes and a towel, so I could take a bath. Before I can even utter a word, Fenna's mom gives me a window cleaner and a cloth. She goes to Fenna and passes her a broom.

"Do I have to?" I ask.

"If you're staying here, you're also doing chores," she says.

"Ugh. Fine."

After I am done cleaning the windows, I give back the cloth.

"Now, what was it that you needed? Was it a towel? Oh, right," she says and hands me a towel.

I go into the bathroom to enjoy a short peaceful bath.

After a while, when we were all taking a break from our chores, I ask, "When should I leave to find Dad?"

"You mean *we*," Kelly says.

"I am also coming," Fenna says.

"Fine. When should *we* leave to find Dad?" I ask.

"Perhaps tomorrow?" Fenna suggests.

"I was thinking of going now, just so that we could finish it off quickly," I say.

"Okay. Sounds good to me. Then we can have endless time to do normal stuff," Fenna says.

As I suggested, we leave right away. We teleport through my powers to Dad's house. Obviously, the house brings back bad memories, but I try my best not to weep in front of the door again.

We barge into the house. The place looks like someone had been there. We check each and every room, but find no one. After we come back downstairs to check the rooms again, I hear the door creak. Fenna quickly goes behind the door as it opens. It's Dad. When he enters, she closes the door behind him. Kelly and I stand cross-armed in front of him. Dad's frightened face tells me he knows what is coming.

"Hello, Danica and Kelly. Where have you been all this time?" he asks.

"I am pretty sure you know where we've been. You're the one who delivered us to him, aren't you?" Kelly asks.

"Who is *him*?" Dad asks, clearly bluffing.

"You know who *he* is!" I say.

"Well, I better go and get changed," he says.

Before he could even move, I freeze his legs and stick them to the ground.

"I don't think you're going anywhere right now," I say.

"Do you, by any chance, happen to know where Mom is?" Kelly asks.

Dad's eyes widen. "Err… She is in…"

"The dead?" I ask.

"Err… Well, we don't have to get to that topic, do we?"

I make the ice on Dad's feet spread all around his body except his head. "I think we do."

"I'd like a really good explanation of why you killed her," I order.

"He threatened to kill me with his death strike if I didn't do as he ordered!" Dad says.

"Kelly, don't you think that is a really good explanation?" I ask her.

"Yeah, good enough to get killed," Kelly says.

"Now kids, I'm pretty sure that isn't necessary," Dad says.

"If you really cared for Mom, for Andy and Archie, and for us, you would have sacrificed yourself instead of even attempting to kill any of us. But, I guess, it is in your selfish personality not to care about anyone but yourself!" I rage.

"Kids, please do not kill me!" Dad says.

"Tell me how you killed my mother, and I might make your death less painful," I order.

He looks at me in despair.

"After you kids disappeared and Jennifer came back home from the waterpark safe but distressed, I decided to lift her mood, and in the process, execute my plan. I told her to meet me at the edge of a cliff. She waited there for me, just as I asked. She didn't suspect a thing. I tried to act normal like everything was fine. I knew it was the last time I would see her. I wanted to spend quality time with her. After some time, I told her one last goodbye and reluctantly pushed her. She fell down and landed in the ocean." A tear runs down his face.

"You vile man! I may as well say that you're worse than Zephyr. He at least cared for Lezabel. You cared for no one," Kelly bellows.

"I guess it is time to kill you now," I say, anger still in my voice. "Let's take you to the edge of a cliff."

I teleport everyone to a cliff. Just to get it over with, before he can even make an expression, I quickly push my father off the cliff. He falls slowly. In a few seconds, he reaches the ocean.

As I see his lifeless body float away into the ocean. I sit down and start crying. My heart hurts, not because I killed my dad, but because he killed my mom. Kelly, trying her best to get over it, comforts me.

We teleport back to Fenna's home.

-21-

Harp

"How are you feeling?" Fenna enters the room to check on me.

"I feel really good."

"I'm really sorry about, well, everything," she says.

"When will we go search for the harp?" I ask, changing the topic.

She gives me a look telling me to get my mind off this Revenir stuff for a bit.

"If you don't want to come, you don't have to!" I remind her.

"I know," she says. "I just want to take a short break. Can't we go after a few days?"

"The thing is, the sooner we lift off the burden, the sooner we can get back to a normal life."

"Are you sure you even want to give these powers up?"

"Stop making me wonder if I should or should not give away my powers. It is making me confused. I might go nuts."

"I just don't want you to let go of these cool powers. I mean, this is any kid's dream — to be able to make water do whatever you want, to be able to shoot lightning from the tip of your fingers, turn into a Pegasus, make your drawings come alive… basically, magic. If you were to travel three years back, don't you think you would love it if you had these powers? You would, wouldn't you? Look, all I am trying to say is, consider your choice. Are you sure?" Fenna says.

We both get a little quiet.

"The thing is, I can't choose. I really love these powers, they're awesome. But, I equally hate what they have done to my life. I am an orphan now." I say. "And, what about the green water human? What if that turns into a bigger problem? Would you like to repeat these two years? I feel the water is a sign that something terrible is coming up. I get the feeling that this terrible thing might be worse than Zephyr."

"But, what if that green water thing still causes a problem? Wouldn't you prefer to have your powers to fight that?"

"I hope it doesn't. I just want to get as far away from all of this as possible. You know what, I am going to leave today; you can come if you want."

"Fine, I too want to get this over with," Fenna says. "But, let's go after lunch, okay? Say, in two hours?"

"Good idea."

We talk about school for a while. Apparently, Fenna's dad is enrolling us girls in a boarding school and the boys in Fenna's old school, since the boarding school starts at seventh grade.

After some time, Fenna leaves the room. I lie in my bed and think. If only I can let go of the thoughts. I don't want to keep dwelling on on them. I try thinking about anything else like where we can search for the harp. How about I try to get Alice to show me where it can be?

'Hey, Alice, can you please show me where the harp is?' I ask her through my mind.

'First, you need to go to sleep, so that I can show it in the form of a dream… How am I speaking to you?' Alice replies.

'You can reply to me. Have you never done that before?'

'Even I didn't know I could do that. Out of all the 347 people I

have been with, you're the first one I can talk to. You must be special, Danica!'

I blush a little.

'Since you can talk to me, can you just tell me where it is?'

'Sure. It is in the Northern Isle. When you reach there, I will guide you further.'

I quickly go out of the room and dash into Fenna's.

"I got news," I say.

"Is it good news?"

"It depends on the way you look at it."

"Wait, call Kelly first."

"Kelly!" I call her, and my throat becomes sore because of my loud voice.

"Yes?" She rushes up.

"Sit down and listen," I order.

"Okay..." Kelly says, still trying to understand what is going on.

"I thought of asking Alice about the whereabouts of the harp, hoping she could show me a vision or a dream. Instead, she spoke to me," I explain. "She told me that the harp is in the Northern Isle."

"Perfect. We leave after lunch?" Fenna asks.

"Yup."

When we are done with lunch, we start getting ready to leave. Kelly gets her origami ninja stars. I try the art shifting power and draw a long, slim sword for Fenna.

"Ready?" I ask.

"Ready." They nod.

All of us take a deep breath, and I teleport everyone to the beach on the island. We start heading for the forest. Before going in, I wonder – do I really want to do this? Then I realise, I don't really have a choice. After saying, "Here goes nothing," we step into the forest.

Unlike the forest in the Southern Isle, this forest has light. The forest also has a soothing temperature. Honestly, it is not what I expected.

Like google maps, Alice keeps on telling me to *'turn right,'* or *'turn left,'* or *'watch out for the trees.'* Wait, what? The trees? Is it the thorns I am watching out for?

When Fenna says, "Uh, guys?" and points at the trees, I realise what Alice meant.

We notice that the trees use their roots as hands. Before we could act, a tree grabs each of us, by twirling its roots around our bodies. I decide it is better to teleport us. The problem is, I am too squished. I don't have enough energy to use my powers.

A thought comes to me. Why would the trees be carrying us? They will have to put us down sometime. The trees can't eat humans; they only consume soil nutrients. Well, the trees might want to kill us because they think of us as foes. Humans have chopped down trees, lots of them. But how are they going to kill us? Are they going to choke us to our death? Not good.

I try finding a way out. There is always a way out. This time, unfortunately, the light bulb in my head won't light. Maybe I can try my powers again. I use all my willpower to make it work, but still nothing. Come on, powers, please work!

I can use the powers I am best at. That is water. How is water going to help? Thankfully, this time, the light bulb lights up. Plants, like every other living organism, have water in them. I can use the water inside them to control their whole body.

First, I need to be able to use my water power at least. For that, the roots have to loosen up a little. Fenna's sword. She throws her sword at me. I am so close to catching the sword, but sadly, I miss it. It starts falling. The good thing is, the sword falls perfectly on one of the roots of the tree. The blade cuts right through the roots. The agony the tree is facing makes the grip of the roots loosen — not enough for me to escape, but enough for me to use my water powers. I use the few seconds I have wisely and start controlling the moving tree. I make it release me on the ground, followed by Kelly and Fenna. We all start walking forward calmly. As I walk, I make the water in each of the trees freeze so they can't attack.

Alice gives me the last instruction. *'Dig the ground.'*

I shapeshift into a badger and start right away. I dig for 10 seconds until I find the harp. The harp radiates a bright glow illuminating illuminating the entire forest. Though it was already bright, the trees had not been. Now, the trees and the atmosphere are glowing as well, with gold dust sparkling everywhere... I quickly finish what I had come for.

'Alice, how does this work?' I ask.

'Just touch the harp for one minute and 20 seconds and release. All your powers will go away,' she replies.

I do exactly as she says. I hold the harp in my hand. Fenna counts down from eighty seconds. When she is done, I let go of the harp. I feel so different — my powers are gone. Its feel like a chunk of me has been lifted. I t can no longer do that cool mind control or the X-ray vision. Most of all, I can't control water anymore. And Alice... Just when we were starting to get to know each other, I had to push her away.

Not able to do it myself, I ask Fenna and Kelly to break the harp. But, apparently, it is impossible to do so. So, instead, we decide to leave it where it was. We cover the harp again, which takes around half an hour.

"How are we going back home, now?" Fenna asks.

"I could telepo... Oh. I don't know," I say.

"Let's first walk out of the forest. We'll figure it out later."

When we are back on the beach, we don't need to figure out a way. I see a white figure coming towards us, from up in the air.

"Is that—" Fenna asks.

"Flake!" I cry.

Flake dashes down quickly when he hears my voice.

He lands in a matter of seconds. Oh, how I missed him. I hug him for two minutes until Kelly says, "Can we start moving?"

Once we all get on, I ask him, "Can you take us to Alenzon, boy?"

"Neigh!" he agrees.

He lifts his front legs as horses do before starting to run. He takes off. We reach home really quickly. After saying my thanks to Flake, and letting him go and spend time with the other Pegasi in town, we go back home.

"Now all my worries have been officially cleared," I say.

"I hope you don't have anything else you want to do because I am not coming with you the next time," Fenna says.

-22-

Mission: School

"Everybody ready?" I ask.

"Yes," Fenna says.

"This is the most dangerous thing we've ever encountered," I say.

"Seriously guys? We're only going to school. I see nothing dangerous in this," Kelly says.

"How don't you find this dangerous?" I ask.

"How do you find this more dangerous than a water park?"

"Okay, fine! The water park is more dangerous! But, school is second dangerous."

"What about the Fotigris? The one that gave you that scar on your leg."

"School will give me the worst pain than a boring scar!"

"Hey, remember when you told me you swore you'd never complain about school again?" Fenna says. "What happened to that?"

"I am not complaining. I am showing how bold and brave I am to go to school," I say.

Kelly rolls her eyes.

"Don't you roll your eyes at me like that."

After half an hour, we reach. There aren't many people here yet. We walk towards the school gates, our Pegasi tailing us. By the gate, two people stand, guarding the gates. They ask for our names.

"I am Kelly Wynter. This is my sister Danica Wynter, and this is Fenna Jockwyn," Kelly says.

"I'd like to see your IDs," the guard says.

We show him the IDs we had received yesterday.

"Welcome to Tarrabelle Academy," he says.

The gates open behind him. He steps aside to let us in.

"Woah!" The school building is huge. Pretty huge. It looks like a big town. Wow, I love this campus.

"It is indeed amazing." Fenna agrees.

A lady comes to us and says, "Welcome to Tarabelle Academy." She checks our IDs. "Follow me, I will escort you to your room where you can settle for a bit."

First, we leave our Pegasi in the stables, where they enjoy among themselves. Then, we go to our own rooms.

Each room is the shape of a hut. Three people stay in one room, which means Fenna, Kelly, and I get to stay in the same room. The lady instructs us to go to the main hall at 2 pm. Then, she leaves.

We enter our hut. It looks really welcoming. There are three different compartments, and it is very spacious. There is one common bathroom. In each compartment, there is a bed, a study desk, and a cupboard. I get the middle compartment. I put my clothes in my cupboard and start setting up my room. On the study desk, there is a cute lamp that looks like a tree. I place a picture of Mom on the table. When we are all done settling everything, we go for a stroll.

We exit the hut. That is when we see him coming. Another lady is escorting Franz to his hut, which is right next to ours. I call out to Franz. We run towards him.

"You're going to the same school, I see." I smile.

"Indeed," he says.

Fenna and Kelly greet him.

"Would you like to come with us?" I ask.

"I'd love to, but I've got to unpack."

"I guess I'll see you around then," I say.

He smiles and enters his hut.

After we unpack our things, settle in, and have a good look around the school, we run to the main hall. The main hall is gigantic. It has rows of seats and something that looks like a stage. The principal of the school, Mr Richard, stands up. We quickly rush to the empty seats.

"Welcome to Tarabelle Academy…" the principal says.

I am not going to tell you the rest of his speech, because you will start snoring before you reach halfway.

After Mr Richard's extremely boring speech, Fenna suggests, "Wanna go to the skating track?"

"Duh, I do!"

We find spare skates of a range of sizes, and each wear a pair that fits. I haven't done skating in quite a long time, so I keep losing my balance and falling.

"One, two, three, go!" I scream.

We dash, as quickly as we can, which is not very fast compared to the last time I went skating. I fall onto my face, giving Fenna an easy win, but she trips over me, hurting me even more. I push Fenna off my back and get up again. Before Fenna can even manage to get on her feet (or her skates), I skate through the finish line.

After a bit more practice, I start grasping the techniques again. Gradually, I get faster at skating. When we are ready to do one more race, I have seized all the skills I had.

"On your marks… Get set… Go!" Fenna yells.

I go way faster than the last race. I finally am able to feel the wind. As I glide, soaring through the wind, I get a sensation of complete freedom.. My soul has been released (quite literally, and figuratively).

As I skate, I realise that magic is found in daily life. I feel like a bird (shapeshifting), flying through the sky.

When I swim, I feel like I control the water (water control). I can communicate with my twin, Kelly, without saying a word (telepathy).

I skate ten times quicker than Fenna. Before I know it, I have crossed the finish line. Fenna is still only halfway done. I wait for her to finish the whole round.

After a while, we go back to the hut. Honestly, today has been a relaxing day.

Since I am completely idle, sitting in the hut, I decide to read through some of the textbooks, so I can understand what we will be learning before we actually start. Don't tell me I have changed immensely because I am already aware. For some reason, I don't mind this change, though.

I find out that the topics we will be learning are really confusing. I have no idea how I will manage the classwork, let alone the homework and extra assignments. I keep revising until my brain feels like it is about to explode.

Someone knocks at our door. Kelly and Fenna are in the adjacent rooms, and so don't hear the knock. I open the door.

"Hi," Franz says. "I thought I'd come to meet you."

"Hey, come in," I say.

He enters the hut.

"So… uhh… how's it going?" He asks.

"First, you tell me," I ask.

"Nothing really. My Dad forced me to study, so I've been reluctantly studying the whole week. I also got a chance to get closer to my parents. My brother had been crying so much. I've seen my mom and brother cry, but my dad… this was the first time," Franz says.

"I didn't even get a reunion with my parents. My mom is dead, so no reunions with her. My dad… well, I killed him," I say.

"You what?"

"He killed my mom; I had no choice!" I say.

"Damn."

"Speaking of killing, I hope I am not bringing up a touchy subject, but what was it like when you were dead?"

"It was amazing. It was a large, and endless space, full of things I only saw in my dreams. All my friends were there, including you. We were all having fun. I sort of wanted to stay there. But then, I felt all of you, strong spirits, were pulling me back to the living."

"That… that is a better afterlife than what I experienced. *Way* better."

"So… Where are the other girls?"

"Kelly! Fenna! We've got a guest!" I scream.

They come dashing out of their rooms.

"What?" Fenna asks. "Oh, hi."

Franz waves.

"What brings you here? Are you ready to annoy us again?" Kelly asks.

"I just came to see you guys."

"Dinner ends at nine. We better hurry if we want a smaller queue," I say.

We walk to the cafeteria. I hadn't noticed how quickly it turned dark and cold. It is much colder than it was earlier.

We grab some food and find a seat.

This is my first meal in this place. The food is delish.

"Delicious pasta," I say, gobbling some cheesy, red pasta.

"So… who is your roommate?" Fenna asks Franz.

"Two boys, not at all my type."

"If you want, you can hang out in our room," I suggest.

"Thanks."

Once we are done eating, we head back to our huts.

"Good night, Franz!"

"Good night!" he replies.

As we enter our hut, I dive into my bed. My muscles aren't tensed, showing how relaxed I am.

Tomorrow is going to be the first day of normal life. I can't wait. Excitement fills my lungs.

The adventures I have had are somewhat extraordinary. I would never want to go back to those scenes, but I have benefitted from them as well. I wouldn't have met Fenna or any of my other friends if it weren't for those adventures. This chunk of my life has been really important to me. It has changed me. The change is for the better or worse, is something that depends on how I view it.

Finally, the war is over.

Evil has fallen.

Peace has triumphed.

But, thinking of what Fenna had said to me earlier and knowing this world as well as I do, I can definitely say, the good hasn't succeeded permanently; it has won temporarily. Someday, someone else might become selfish and plan to destroy the world for their own entertainment. But, at least, I can live a normal life now.

Acknowledgements

A big thank you to all the readers who picked up my book. I am so glad I got to share this book with you guys, and I'm even happier you all decided it was worth your time. I hope you guys loved this book as much as I loved writing it.

To NuVoice Press and HubHawks team, thank you for helping share my dream with the world! I am forever grateful for all of your effort in the cover illustration, editing the book, publishing it (of course), and the marketing. It has been an enormous pleasure working with you.

To Falguni Jain, I would like to share my gratitude for the amazing editing done on your part. It was wonderful to see the improvement in my book that you helped with. Thank you so much!

To my extremely annoying yet adorable little brother, I truly loved how interested you were in my book. I was reluctant to show my book to anyone before it came out, but you begged me to the point where I couldn't refuse anymore. I loved seeing you as engrossed in something I had written, as you are in the comics you love reading. Thank you for being my Number 1 fan, Nabz.

To mumma and papa, thank you for always believing in me. I remember being excited to tell you that I had started writing a book and was even more thrilled when I finished it. Ever since I finished my book, you haven't missed any opportunity to remind me of how proud you are, and I absolutely love it when you tell me that. Not only have you helped and supported me emotionally, but also worked so hard to find editors and publishers. I don't know how to thank you enough. Thank you, guys, I love you so much.

To Dadu and Bhua, thank you for always introducing my book to guests, family members, and all the people you met. It made me feel seen and appreciated every time you guys brought it up. I am so glad you guys passed down the writing gene to me. Thank you for showing so much excitement for my book.

To Marm and Fatima, who were the entire reason I even started writing this book in the first place. It was so motivating to know that you guys were also writing books (though you were infuriatingly faster). We started our books during the coronavirus lockdown, and it was fun having this little project we did together. I remember suggesting publishing our books, and we all were so excited to do so, despite the fact that we all knew deep down that it was never going to happen. It's ironic that three years later, I've managed to reach the point where I am writing 'Acknowledgements', and I wouldn't have done it without the Wiggly Triplets.

To all of my closest friends (you know who you guys are), I love you all so much. The way some of you were fighting over who read my draft first really made me feel proud, knowing my book was worth fighting over. The way you guys labelled me as the writer of the group made me realise what an amazing achievement this book is. Thank you, guys, for always being my best friends.

To all my cousins, I will gladly give you autographed copies. I just need my hundred million first.

To all of my family, Bindass, and everyone else who showed an interest in my book. Every time you asked when my book would be published, it showed me how excited you were for it. It brought a smile to my face and colour to my cheeks every. Thank you all for those little boosts of motivation.

To anyone I may have forgotten to mention, I am truly sorry. Please blame my terrible memory. I am grateful for whatever way you helped me in this journey. So, thanks a lot.

I am extremely grateful that I had the help and support of so many amazing people. I could never have reached this point without you. Once again, thank you all for making my dream possible.

About the Author

Manya Bhansali is a young and promising author hailing from Surat, India, and currently residing in Dubai. At just age 14, Manya has already established herself as an avid reader with a special interest in fictional genres such as fantasy and murder mystery novels. Her relentless curiosity and profound love for literature distinguish her as an emerging talent in the literary world.

She is an IGCSE Year 11 student at Gems Founders School in Dubai. In addition to her literary achievements, Manya is an accomplished athlete and also a skilled swimmer. Her dedication to sports showcases her discipline and determination – traits that she brings to all aspects of her life.

Manya's writing reflects her unique perspective and vibrant youthful energy. Her work is a blend of imaginative storytelling and insightful themes, marking her as a promising young writer.